A bullet split the air over her head...

Delilah threw herself flat and waited. After what seemed like an age she began to move, dragging herself along the ground, edging her way back to her car.

She started to pull herself upright when the gun banged again. A streak of flame seared her arm.

She screamed and fell—desperately trying to stay conscious. She scrambled away from the menacing sound of the footsteps that came inexorably closer.

Maxine O'Callaghan
Is also the author
of Raven House Mystery #28
Death Is Forever

Delilah West was a broken woman....

Her world had been smashed to
pieces when she found her husband
shot and bleeding to death on the
beach near her home. Obsessed by
revenge, she combed southern
California for the killer, and one day
she found him.

But she was too late.

Someone else had found him first.

Someone else had killed him.

RUN FROM NIGHTMARE

Maxine O'Callaghan

A RAVEN HOUSE MYSTERY FROM
WORLDWIDE
TORONTO · LONDON · NEW YORK

First Printing February 1981

ISBN 0-373-60046-1

Printed in Canada

1

I PARKED BEHIND MY OFFICE BUILDING about two o'clock that Wednesday afternoon, peeled my legs off the vinyl seats and slammed the door with relief. Somewhere this late September afternoon was brisk and cool, full of swirling leaves and hints of winter. In southern California the Santa Ana winds screamed down the mountains, honing the air to sinus-crackling clarity and sucking the remaining moisture from dry grass and scorched brush on the hillsides.

I picked my way across the garbage-strewn alley, ducked into the back entrance and headed straight for the soft-drink machine that whined in a dark corner. It gulped four quarters before it grudgingly rattled a Coke can down the chute. I wrapped my hands around the icy aluminum as I climbed upstairs and thought longingly of my cool office.

Beneath the faded gold-leaf lettering on my door that reads West and West Detective Agency, the custodian had scotch-taped a warning: No air-conditioning. Overloaded circuits.

I dug out my key and opened the door, muttering profanities at the useless window unit that cut off any hope of a breeze.

Fifteen minutes, I promised myself, propping open the door. Even my two-finger typing ought to finish the report in that length of time, and then I could get the hell out of here.

I kicked off my shoes, stripped off my panty hose and dug out a pair of sandals I keep in the bottom desk drawer, wondering why I'd bothered to dress up. A tailored skirt and blouse might be appropriate attire for getting statements from doctors on a personal-injury suit, but the receptionists who politely took the checks and informed me that "Doctor's busy right now," were not impressed.

Holding the cold can against my forehead, I picked up the telephone and dialed my answering service.

"Rita?" I propped the phone between my ear and shoulder and broke a fingernail prying up the tab on my cola. "Ouch, dammit . . . it's Delilah."

"Is that any indication of the way your day is going?"

"Pretty close." I took a long, cooling swallow. "Any messages?"

"No, but . . . Delilah? Are you going to be there for a while?"

"Just long enough to finish a report."

"Will you wait for me? I'll leave right away. I need to talk to you."

"Come to my apartment. I have visions of cold drinks and cold salads."

"No, kiddo, I can't. It's. . . ." She hesitated. "Well, it's business. Your kind of business. Can't talk now. There's another call. See you in half an hour."

"Rita?" I began, but she disconnected the line.

Weird, I thought as I slowly recradled the phone.

I drank half the can of Coke and wondered about Rita Braddock. Ours had been strictly a business relationship until my husband, Jack, the other half of West and West Detective Agency, was killed. Jack was an orphan, my immediate family was dead and most of our friends were scattered. I had needed somebody desperately. There was a big hole in my life, and Rita did her best to fill it. We became closer than friends. She was more like family. I clenched my fists as a painful tide of memories swept me back to that black, bitter time.... It took an enormous effort to pull my thoughts away.

How much did I really know about Rita? Basic statistics, of course. She was in her mid fifties, lived in a one-room apartment behind her office and was as much alone as I was. She spoke only once about her ex-husband. Tersely she described how he deserted her and their five-year-old son, lived a short, alcoholic life and died in the gutter. The boy, Michael, had been killed in Vietnam. She mentioned a sister who lived back east, but I got the impression they weren't close.

Friends? Enemies? Lovers? I ought to know, I told myself, remembering with a twinge of guilt how long it had been since I had made an effort to see her.

These past months I'd been like some terrified creature, inching its way out of a hole, too wrapped up in my own pain to notice anybody else. What had happened to Rita during that time? Why did she need a private detective?

It was useless to speculate. I'd know soon enough. Meanwhile I dug out my notes, cranked a sheet of paper into the typewriter and stared at it morosely. Twenty minutes later I ripped the report out of the typewriter, scrawled my signature at the bottom of the page and stuffed it into an envelope.

"Thank God," I said and tilted the last of the Coke into my mouth. It was lukewarm and sticky-sweet, but I drank it anyway.

Just as I dropped the can into the wastebasket, Rita walked through the door.

"Jesus," she said. "You planning to grow orchids in here? I thought you had the air conditioner fixed."

"I did, but . . . ah, the hell with it."

I went over and punched the "on" button. The unit whined sluggishly to life and cool air drifted from the vents.

Rita closed the door and sat down across the desk from me. Graying red hair, cropped short, curled around her freckled, square face. She had long since come to terms with the fact that her size six-teen derriere would never fit into size ten designer jeans, so she was sensibly dressed in a wrap skirt and a blouse that was large enough not to strain over her breasts.

"I'm sure you're wondering why I called this meeting," she said with a nervous grin.

"The thought did occur to me."

"I want you to find somebody, Delilah. Her name is Janet Valek and she—"

"No!" Panic gripped me as I remembered the last time I'd gone to look for a girl, a simple missing persons case that turned into a nightmare of death. "No, Rita. I don't take cases like that anymore."

"I noticed. You've been hiding out here for months behind a lot of dull routine."

"I like it," I muttered.

"Crap. You're running scared."

"Diplomacy was always your finest quality."

She ignored my remark. "Delilah, I know you

went through hell when Jack was murdered. You blamed yourself for his death. But you never gave up until you found his killer.''

"Oh, yeah, I was brilliant."

"Kiddo, it's over and done with. It's time you got on with your work. I need you, and dammit," she added sharply, "you owe me one.''

She was right about that. Her loyalty had kept me out of jail long enough to finish that investigation—to expiate my guilt. What else could I say? "All right, Rita, I'll listen. But no promises."

She took a deep breath. "My son, Michael, was engaged to Janet Valek. It wasn't that I didn't like the girl, but it seemed to me she'd had too much money and not enough love. I thought Mike was headed for trouble.''

"Did you say anything to him?"

"Me? Of course. Mike told me to mind my own business. Anyway, maybe it would have worked out but Mike died and. . . ." She looked away, into the past, for a long, sad moment.

"Janet and I were close for a while," she went on. "Afterward we stayed in touch. You know—Christmas, birthdays, lunch now and then. Anyway, I hadn't heard from her for a long time and then she forgot my birthday. So, big deal, but she always sends me a card, something special; she's that kind of a girl, she goes to a lot of trouble to pick it out. Well, it bothered me, so a couple of weeks later I called to make sure she was okay. The maid told me that she was out of town."

"She went on vacation and it slipped her mind," I said, wondering where all this was leading.

"I figured it that way until her brother called. He's been in Europe all summer. Janet knew he'd be home for two weeks before school started, but she's still gone and nobody seems to know where she went. He's crazy with worry.''

"Maybe she found a boyfriend who interests her more than a brother.''

"Not Janet. She was fourteen when David was born. Their mother died a year later and Janet practically raised the boy. He just finished his first year of college and Janet really missed him. If she wasn't going to be home, she would at least call.''

"Okay, let's backtrack. Does Janet live alone?''

"She lives with her father over in Newport Beach.''

"Is he worried about her?''

"No, but that doesn't mean much.''

"I take it you're not fond of Mr. Valek?''

"He's the biggest bastard I ever met and that's saying a lot.''

"Okay, forget Valek. The maid told you that Janet went out of town. That doesn't sound as though she vanished. Did she pack a bag? Take her car?''

"Yes, but—''

"When?''

"In June, right after David left for Europe.''

"Was he home then? Did he talk to her?''

"I don't know. I don't think so, but—'' She looked at her watch. "You can ask David yourself. He's meeting me here in a few minutes.''

"You had all this planned, didn't you?''

"Don't be mad, kiddo. David sounded so upset, and I knew if anybody could help him it was you. Besides,'' she added briskly, "it's time you got off your butt and started doing your job. What else do you need? A description?''

"Why not?"

"She's a couple of years older than you . . . about thirty-two. Five feet six inches, dark blond hair—wait a minute. You met her."

"I did?"

"Sure. At South Coast Plaza about a year ago. Remember?"

I did, sort of. I had been working as a sales clerk at one of the posh department stores in the mall, an undercover assignment to investigate some inside theft. With the job successfully completed, I decided to break pita bread and share alfalfa sprouts with the Gucci set at Forty Carrots. The encounter in the restaurant with Rita and Janet had been brief, but now I had a hazy memory of a slender, elegant girl—thin face, almost gaunt, hair the color of amber honey pulled back simply with combs from a wide forehead. And there was something about her eyes. . . .

The memory faded abruptly as my office door swung open. The man who stalked in was much too old to be Janet's younger brother. He radiated more brute power than I had ever seen. His lightweight silk suit had been cleverly tailored to disguise a stomach bulge and his thinning gray hair was carefully arranged to cover a receding hairline. From the expression of disgust on Rita's face, I had a pretty good idea who he was.

A younger man followed a few steps behind, catching the door before it slammed in his face. This had to be David. Except for his dark brown hair, the resemblance to Janet was startling. The same face, angled and textured by masculinity, and, although there was nothing feminine about his slender, bony body, there was something of Janet's casual elegance in the way he moved.

The older man loomed over my desk, raking Rita with pale blue eyes before giving me the full benefit of their icy anger. "I'm Lawrence Valek. I understand my son has some crazy idea about hiring you to find his sister."

"He overheard me talking to you," David said to Rita. "He insisted on coming along."

Valek wheeled on him. "Don't talk behind my back. That's what started this whole thing. And you, Mrs. Braddock—I'll thank you to stop meddling in my family's affairs."

"Meddling?" Hard red spots colored Rita's cheeks. "David's worried about Janet; so am I. It seems pretty strange to me that you're so unconcerned."

Before the reply that rumbled in Valek's throat could explode, I put in quickly, "Let's sit down and talk about it."

I hauled over a couple of chairs from the far wall. David accepted with a grateful smile. Valek eyed the room contemptuously before he sat down. I was instantly aware of the broken window shade and the dust balls in the corners. I tried to hide my bare legs behind the desk.

"David, Mr. Valek, I'm Delilah West. If we could just discuss this calmly—"

"We won't discuss it at all," Valek said. "I came here to put a stop to this nonsense."

"Dad, please. It's not like Janet to act this way."

"It's exactly like her. She's thoughtless, cruel. . . and this. . . this *farce* is typical."

"Mr. Valek," I said soothingly, "your son strikes me as a reasonable person. I know Rita is. If we can come up with some logical explanation of Janet's behavior, I'm sure they'll accept it. Now, as I understand it, David was away when Janet left. Did she discuss her plans with you?''

"She did not. She simply packed a bag and left, as usual. This isn't the first time she's gone off without a word. She does it all the time.''

"Well, if you wouldn't fight with her—''

"David, that's enough.''

"No, it's not." David faced him squarely; it was Valek's eyes that shifted away. "They're always fighting, Mrs. West. It's awful. Sometimes Janet just has to go away to cool off.''

So maybe Valek was right and Rita and David were worrying over nothing. "These other times when Janet went away," I said, "did she call you, David, let you know where she was?''

"Not always," he admitted. "Anyway, I wasn't here this summer so—''

"So she couldn't call you," I finished and turned to Valek. "Did you and Janet have a fight?''

"No.''

"David, did you talk to her before you left for Europe?''

"Yes. She sounded sort of jumpy and—I don't know—strained. We've always been very close and I knew something was bothering her, but I thought it was because I was going to Europe without coming home first. When I think that she could be alone and sick somewhere, or...or even... dead.''

"This is ridiculous," Valek said. "You don't think I'd let her go off without finding out exactly where she went?''

"Why, you bastard!" Rita exploded. "You let this kid worry himself sick and didn't say a word?''

"Mrs. Braddock, I told you before to mind your

own business. Your connection with my family ended a long time ago . . . fortunately.''

"Dad!" David said, appalled. "Rita, he didn't
mean—''

"Oh, yes, he did." The stricken look on Rita's
face quickly turned back to rage.

I got around the desk and grabbed her shoulder.
"Rita, take it easy. I'm sure he didn't mean it the
way it sounded.''

"Oh, he meant it all right," Rita said, standing up.
"I've got to get out of here, Delilah. Call me when
you talk to Janet, will you, David?''

"Sure, Mrs. Braddock." David walked her to the
door and squeezed her hand. "Thanks.''

I sat down behind my desk and stared into
Lawrence Valek's eyes. They had the same cold
flatness I'd once seen in the eyes of a boa constric-
tor at the zoo. I tried to think of a way to get him
out of my office and fast.

"This is obviously a family matter," I said. "Why
don't you two go home and—''

"Dad." Ignoring me, David stood behind a chair,
gripping the back. "I'm not going back to school
next week unless you tell me where Janet is.''

"What?" Valek almost strangled on the word.

"I'll find her myself. Or I'll get a job and hire
somebody to do it for me.''

"David, why are you doing this?" A kind of
pathetic bewilderment replaced the arrogance on
Valek's face. "I'm trying to protect you; I've always
tried to protect you.''

David remained silent, unmovable.

"You're getting to be more and more like *her*,"
Valek said bitterly. "All right, I'll tell you. She went
off with a man. This one's even worse than usual.

Evidently she can't tear herself away from him long enough to come and see you. I'm not going to tell you where she is because I won't have you mixed up in one of her sordid messes.''

"Then don't tell me. Tell Mrs. West.''

"Now wait a minute," I said.

"Please, Mrs. West. Just go and make sure Janet's okay. That's all I'm asking you to do.''

It seemed a simple enough request. God knows I didn't want his father for a client, but how could I say no to David? Or to Rita?

Still, I wished I'd never met Janet Valek. Because now, looking at her brother, I remembered distinctly; especially her eyes. . .unusual eyes. . .a soft blue, smudged with violet. There was something familiar about them.

With a start I realized they reminded me of my own, which was crazy because mine are brown, nothing at all like Janet's. . .except for a shadow of something dark and painful moving behind the surface.

One thing was certain. I didn't want to know what haunted Janet Valek.

2

I MADE ONE LAST FEEBLE ATTEMPT to get out of the job. "David, your father might have somebody on retainer who can do this."

"I don't want anybody else. I want you. Please, Dad?" The pleading in his voice was that of a small boy.

For an instant the old man's face softened. He nodded and said gruffly, "Wait for me in the car."

What could I do but say yes?

As soon as David closed the door behind him, Valek took out his checkbook. "Let's get one thing straight, Mrs. West. You're working for me and I expect anything I tell you to be confidential."

"For two hundred and fifty dollars a day and expenses, it will be."

He didn't believe me for a minute. "Keep in mind that I have a lot of friends who can see to it that your license gets pulled if it isn't."

So much for his show of human emotions. Somehow I liked it better when I could think of him as a coldhearted son of a bitch.

I SAT ALONE in my office listening to the air conditioner wheeze. After all the storm and thunder, the facts in the case were simple. Janet was living with an artist named Felix Bak in Oro, a town located less than fifty miles away inland, on the other side of the Santa Ana Mountains.

I knew the place. It had been founded a long time ago by some hopeful prospector. Although gold had been discovered farther south in the Lagunas, as far as I know Oro never lived up to its name. Until a few years ago, rattlesnakes had outnumbered the people. Now the construction of Interstate 15 carved an intermittent path from Riverside to San Diego, passing on the outskirts of town.

Valek didn't have a telephone number or an address for Bak.

"No phone," he had told me. "No proper address, either. Just a post-office box. He lives in a shack in a place called Mesquite Canyon, miles from town."

I looked at my watch. There was still time to drive to Oro. It was a small town; somebody would know where Felix Bak lived. If I hurried, David could be talking to his sister tonight.

Of course, it was almost five o'clock. By the time I went home, ate dinner and drove there, it would be dark. Silly to go stumbling around looking for Bak's remote house in the middle of the night. Better to wait until morning.

Better not to go at all.

This is stupid, I told myself, picking up Valek's check and putting it in my purse. And this was an easy job, easy money. I didn't even have to track the girl down.

Reason helped me to ignore the little worm of dread that wriggled deep inside. Logic marched me through the routine of closing the office, driving home, cooking a TV dinner and eating without tasting it.

After that I prowled the apartment, lifting the

telephone and dropping it back without dialing. I
need more time, I thought desperately. It's too
soon. Damn you, Rita. I can't handle it.

I felt like I'd just crawled off an operating table. A
big hunk of my insides had been cut away and the
suturing was only half-finished. I stumbled into the
bedroom and took Jack's picture from the drawer
of my bedside table. For a long time I sat, huddled,
in the middle of my bed, holding the picture until
the pain stopped. It left me numb and empty, thinking only of sleep.

For a long time after Jack's death as soon as I
closed my eyes the nightmares began. Now, I never
dream. . . or if I do I don't remember it. Sleep is my
escape from reality.

I put Jack's picture away, got into a nightgown
and crawled back into bed. Immediately I fell into a
deep, black, paralyzing void.

The buzzer on the downstairs door startled me
awake. Sunlight flooded the room. I squinted at
the clock. 9:12. I'd slept right through the
alarm. The buzzer squawked nonstop until I lurched
into the living room and punched the intercom button.

"Who is it?"

"Who do you think?" Rita demanded. "I figured
you'd still be here. You gonna leave me standing
down here or what?"

"No," I said wearily. "Come on up."

My body ached from lying in bed so long, but per-
versely all I wanted to do was lie down again. I
leaned against the wall until Rita banged on the
door.

"You look terrific," she said. "How much em-
balming fluid did they use?"

"Gimme a break," I muttered. "Everybody over-sleeps now and then."

"It had nothing to do with your job?"

"No," I lied. "David called and filled you in?"

"He said his father agreed to tell you where Janet was. I suppose you're not going to tell me anything?"

"I can't. You want to bug me some more or would you put on the coffee while I shower?"

"Okay. But don't fall asleep in there."

It was a temptation but I resisted. I dressed in the thinnest, coolest dress I owned and headed for the kitchen. Rita poured me a mug of coffee and went back to stirring eggs. I drank deeply and thought I might live until she slapped a plate in front of me.

"Good God," I exclaimed. "How many did you scramble?"

"Four. You need your strength. Eat."

I rearranged the yellowish mass with a fork. "Rita, why did Janet live at home? With a father like that, you'd think she would have run away when she was a lot younger, say about eight."

"I don't know. Even though we were close after Mike's death, I didn't feel I could ask."

"What do you know about Lawrence Valek?"

"Enough. When Mike and Janet got engaged, I did some checking. You'd never guess it from his snooty attitude, but his folks were a bunch of Okies, same as mine, who moved out to California during the depression. After the war he went into con-struction. He made a buck or two on the G.I. hous-ing boom, but nothing big. As a matter of fact, in the early sixties he almost went under. But then he got some state contract—mental hospital, I think it was—and Valek Construction suddenly hit the big time."

"Let me guess. He made his fortune by being sweet and charming."

"Ha, very funny. No, Valek owes it all to a helpful friend. Remember Daniel Hodge?"

"The state senator who went to jail?"

She nodded. "That's him. I never could figure their connection. Valek's a social climber. Hodge comes from old Orange County money. He was well on his way in politics before he met Valek. The two of them must have milked the state for millions. Remember the big scandal a couple of years ago?"

"I don't remember Valek's being involved."

"He covered his tracks too well. Hodge wasn't so lucky, or so smart. Still, the only charge that stuck was misuse of campaign funds."

"Nice fellows." I picked up my plate, took it over to the sink and scraped the uneaten eggs into the garbage disposal. "I think I've lost my appetite. Anyway, I'd better get going."

"You're not taking a suitcase," she observed. "It must be someplace close by."

"Rita—"

"Okay, okay. I won't ask." She headed for the door, stopped. "You do think Janet's all right, don't you, kiddo?"

"Yes. By tomorrow you'll all be happy as clams and Lawrence Valek will be suing me for a refund."

After she left, I stood uncertainly in the middle of the floor. Of course it would be quick and easy. The hardest part of the job would be the long hot drive back and forth to Oro. I'd be home sipping margaritas before the sun went down. Still, it never hurt to be prepared.

I went into the bedroom and packed an overnight bag. . .just in case. I wouldn't let myself answer the obvious question: just in case of *what*?

THE TWO HIGHEST PEAKS of the Santa Ana Mountains form a distinctive saddle over five thousand feet high. Only one road snakes across the rocky barrier of the range that extends from Central Orange County to Oceanside. I didn't have time for this scenic route. I drove up the Riverside Freeway, circling behind the mountains on Route 71. By the time I got to Oro, sweat glued my dress to my back and my eyes stung. Smoke cast a yellow pall over the hard blue skies from brush fires that raged from Los Angeles to San Diego—seven at last count, according to the radio. I could see three of them blackening the horizon.

A sign just inside Oro's city limits gave the population (5,000), the altitude (550 feet), listed meeting days for the Kiwanis and promised that the town was progressive and friendly.

Evidently the attendant at the service station across the street had never read the sign. He ignored me when I tooted the horn, so I got out and rapped on the locked glass-panel door. He was having lunch and doing some heavy reading. After a minute of persistent knocking he put down his Bud and his copy of *Porno Illustrated* and stomped over.

"What the hell's the matter with you, lady? Can't you read? Sign says we're outta gas."

"I need some directions."

"Maps are a dollar. Over there in the vending machine. I don't make change."

"This is local. Can you tell me how to find Mesquite Canyon?"

"Never heard of it."

"How about Felix Bak? He's a painter. Have you heard of him?"

"Oh, yeah. I saw a couple of his paintings down at the bank. Modern junk, but I hear his private collection ain't half bad." He grinned wolfishly and reevaluated my body. "You his new model?"

"Not if I can't find him." I smiled. I have to smile at a lot of people I don't like. "Where does he live?"

"Out toward the Adams's ranch. Go through town, take the last street on the left. Three or four miles out, hang a right. You sure you got to rush off?"

Before the lechery in his mind could make the slow connection with his meaty hands, I backed away, mumbling, "Thanks," and got into my car.

The main street in Oro played its gold rush ancestry to the hilt with false fronts, wooden sidewalks and hitching rails. It was almost twelve o'clock and the Gold Pan Café and Saloon tempted me briefly, but I decided to look for Mesquite Canyon first.

After I made the turn as directed, the paved street quickly left civilization, turned to gravel and then to dirt. An hour of dust, potholes and wrong turns brought me back to my starting point on the edge of town. I pulled over and parked. Obviously, I was going to need something better than the service-station attendant's directions.

I was turning over the possibilities when I saw the woman. I'd stopped in front of the last house on the street, a small adobe structure set in the middle of a Bermuda lawn that was turning brown in the heat. It was a twin to the house next door, down to the row of eucalyptus shading the southern exposure and the thicket of oleander lining long, narrow driveways that led to garages in back. The woman sat in a lawn chair near the front door, face turned to the sun.

I left my car and walked toward her, already having second thoughts. Anybody who sat, fully dressed, in this heat probably had fried their brains and couldn't even point out the general direction of Los Angeles, but I figured I might as well try.

There was no sidewalk, so I walked on the graveled edge of the asphalt for a few feet to reach the driveway, then cut across the grass.

"Jannie," the woman called eagerly. "Jannie?" The expectation turned to uncertainty. "Who is it? Who's there?"

She picked up something lying beside her chair and stood up. It was a white cane.

She was about sixty years old, dressed in a sleeveless print that zipped up the front. A gold charm on a slender chain hung around her neck and caught the sunlight. Thin gray hair was combed back into an untidy bun. Sweat glossed her lined, anxious face and the eyes she turned on me were empty.

"I'm sorry," I said. "I didn't mean to startle you. I got lost and needed directions."

"I'm afraid I can't help. I lost my sight right after we moved here."

"How about next door? Can they—"

"No." She took several anxious steps toward me. "No, nobody's there."

"I'll ask around town, then. Thanks."

She turned and felt her way back to the chair. As she lowered her body, the aluminum frame began tipping to one side. I ran over and grabbed it.

"Careful," I warned.

"Why, thank you." She gave me an embarrassed smile. "I usually take better care of myself."

"Wouldn't you like to go inside? It's pretty hot out here."

"I know. People think I'm crazy. My son's always

warning me to stay out of the heat. But I live in a dark world, and sometimes I just have to feel the sun on my face.''

"I don't think you're crazy." Her hands were clasped on top of the cane. I reached out and touched them as I said goodbye.

I got back in my car and headed into town. I was hot and thirsty and I figured I might as well ask directions in the Gold Pan Café.

Everybody in town must have decided to eat lunch out along with all the tourists from Interstate 15. The parking lot was crowded and there was a wait for a table. I added my name to the list and said I'd be in the bar. Antique instruments for prying gold from the earth shared the walls with tintypes and wanted posters. Rough-sawn wood furniture, smoky beamed ceilings, the recorded tinny piano that plinked in the background—all of it was like oversweet frosting on stale cake.

I took a stool at the bar and glanced at my reflection in the wavy mirror. Not too bad; nothing five or six hours in a beauty salon couldn't fix.

"What'll you have?" The bartender had suspenders holding up his pants and garters pushing back his sleeves.

"Just ginger ale with a lot of ice." When he put it in front of me, I took a long swallow before I said, "Maybe you can help me. I'm looking for Felix Bak. He lives out in Mesquite Canyon. Do you know him?"

"Not personally." He mopped dribbles of carbonated foam from the plastic-coated wood. "I know who he is. Let's see. Mesquite Canyon. I think it's west of town, but I'm new here. Why don't you ask at the gas station?"

"I did. That's why I'm here." As long as he seemed willing to uphold the town's reputation for friendliness, I tried another question. "Do you know Janet Valek?"

"Janet? Oh, sure, Janet comes in all the time . . . or at least she did. I haven't seen her for a while. Why don't you talk to her boss?"

"Who's that?"

"Claire Ingram. Sitting right over there."

"What kind of business is she in?"

"Real estate. She and Philip Hunter are developing a piece of land south of town."

"Thanks." I put a ten-dollar bill on the bar. "Keep the change."

Claire Ingram sat at a corner table, talking earnestly to an older couple. Customers, I thought. I wouldn't endear myself to her if I interrupted her sales pitch. I picked up my ginger ale, moved to the table next to them and waited.

It's hard to estimate age under soft lighting. I guessed Claire was in her late thirties. A cotton knit dress outlined a skinny, Coppertoned body. Her brown hair, carefully streaked and swirled, lay closely against a narrow head.

I caught snatches of the conversation. Terms like "tax write-offs," "hedge against inflation" and "a can't-lose investment" were repeated at frequent intervals. Heady stuff, but it didn't have time to work, because a tall man zigzagged his way through the room and poured himself into the empty chair next to Claire.

"Why'd you sneak off without me?" he asked in a loud, aggrieved voice. He tried to fingercomb his black hair out of his eyes, but it kept falling back. "I never got to say hi to the Smiths. Hi, Grace. Hi,

Harry. What are you drinking? Let's have another round."

I could hear Claire's swift intake of breath and her "For Christ's sake, Philip," before she regained her composure. She got Grace and Harry out of their chairs before Philip could untangle his feet and ushered them toward the dining room with frantic gestures to the hostess.

I wondered if it was safer to introduce myself before or after Claire got in her licks on Philip. While I decided, she stormed back to the table.

"Philip, what's the matter with you? It's bad enough I have to close your deals for you; now you come along and screw things up all over again."

Philip buried his head in his hands. His words were incomprehensible, but Claire's were loud and clear. "Damn that little bitch. I'm glad she's gone. You'll be a lot better off, Philip, if you forget about Janet."

Janet—gone—the temperature in my vicinity dropped several degrees. I gripped the edge of the table, fighting a wild desire to run out of the room and drive straight back to Santa Ana.

Stop it, I told myself. She probably went home.

I pictured happy reunions in Newport Beach and slowly unclenched my fingers. All I had to do was check it out with Claire and Philip and be on my way. I got up and covered the few steps to their table.

"We're in trouble, big trouble, Philip, and unless you—"

"Excuse me," I said.

"What do you want?" Claire demanded. Up close the tan looked more like a second-degree burn and the fashionably thin body was stringy and tough.

"I'm looking for Janet Valek," I said. "I understand she works for you."

"Janet—you know Janet?" Philip attempted to stand up but Claire grabbed his arm.

"Sit down, you fool, before you fall on your face. Are you a friend of hers?" Claire asked me.

"Friend of a friend. I heard you say Janet's gone. Did she go home?"

"How should I know? You don't think she gave me notice? Not that one. Just up and left. Things are in such a mess, I still don't have the filing straightened out."

"Still?" I felt cold again. "When did she leave?"

"Three weeks ago."

"Don't listen to her." Drunken grief ravaged Philip's face. "Janet didn't leave. She vanished. Oh, God," he said brokenly. "She's gone and I'm afraid I'll never see her alive again."

3

"STOP IT, PHILIP," Claire said. "Get hold of yourself."

His words had set off all the alarms in my brain. It was starting again, another cycle of death. I was too late... always too late....

I can't let this case get to me like this, I thought as I drew a deep breath and willed the quivering in my knees to stop. "What's happened to make you think Janet is dead?" I asked Philip.

"Nothing," Claire put in. "He doesn't know what he's saying. Come on, Philip. I'll take you home. Maybe if I hurry back I can salvage the deal with the Smiths."

"Just a minute," I said. "That was a serious charge he made. I want an answer from him."

"You're awfully good at asking questions." Claire eyed me suspiciously. "Exactly who are you?"

"Delilah West. I'm a private investigator." I hated the commitment the words implied, but I had taken Lawrence Valek's money. There was no way out.

"Investigator?" Philip stared at me. He seemed a lot more sober than he had a minute ago. "Somebody hired you to look for Janet?"

"Not exactly. Her father knew where she was, but he hasn't heard from her in a while. I just came to check up on things."

"Thank God," Philip said. "Thank God you're here. Nobody believes me, but I know something terrible has happened to Janet. I didn't know who to notify, who to tell. . . ."

"Philip, will you please stop that crazy—" Claire broke off and stared over my shoulder at the front door. "Oh, God, the Smiths are leaving. I'd better go see what's wrong."

After she hurried away, Philip pleaded, "You do believe me?"

"I don't know what to believe. Do the police know about your suspicions?"

"Yes, I told them—I tried to tell them. They said she left of her own . . . volition." He tasted the word bitterly.

Maybe she did, I thought. Just like she left Newport Beach.

"Janet's leaving must have been a shock for you," I said. "But why do you think she's dead?"

"Because she wouldn't just leave. Because—" He pressed his fingertips against his temples. "Dammit, my head is pounding so badly I can't think straight."

Just then Claire came back and slumped down in a chair. "Well, that tears it. Mr. Smith got an allergy attack. Something in the damn salad dressing. Now he's wheezing and coughing and—God! This whole day has been a total disaster." Her reddish brown eyes told me it was all my fault. "Are you through giving Philip the third degree?"

"I've barely started."

"Well, it'll have to wait. He's in no condition to answer any more questions."

"I just need a shower," Philip said. "A couple of aspirins. Maybe some black coffee."

"How about you, Miss Ingram?" I asked.

She looked at me speculatively and shrugged. "Why not? Yes, as a matter of fact, I would like to talk to you. Why don't you meet me at my office in an hour? I have to take Philip home."

"No, you don't," Philip objected. "I have my car. I'll drive myself. See?" He demonstrated how steady he was on his feet. "I'm all right."

"Well, I'll follow you just to make sure." She glanced at her watch. "Two o'clock, Miss West. Rancho del Oro, just south of town. You can't miss it."

She grabbed Philip's arm and hustled him out. He walked a fairly straight line to the door. I sat there and felt the panic rising. Quickly I pushed it down. I'd do exactly what I had been hired to do. I'd talk to Claire Ingram and Philip Hunter. Maybe to Felix Bak. I'd get the police version of what had happened. Then I'd take it all to Lawrence Valek and let him handle it. There was no reason not to do that much.

The police first, I thought, but just then the hostess clip-clopped over in her cowboy boots. "Mrs. West? Your table's ready."

The cardinal rule for a P.I. is eat when you can; you may not get a chance later.

I followed her swinging denim skirt to a corner booth and accepted a menu. It was varnished wood embossed with an imprint from a branding iron. The price for a meal was more than most cowpokes had made in a week. I was glad Lawrence Valek was paying the bill.

"Cocktail?" she asked.

I never drink at lunchtime.

"Vodka and tonic," I said.

IT WAS ALMOST TWO O'CLOCK when I left the restaurant and drove south. I had wound up having two drinks before lunch and I felt a lot more optimistic than I had earlier.

I know you, Janet Valek, I thought. We're a lot alike, you and me. We just have different ways of running.

I passed a Riverside county sheriff's substation outside of town and made a note of the location for later. Then I hit open country, rolling hills covered with dry grass that looked ready to ignite in the fierce afternoon sun.

I began to wonder about Claire's directions when a huge sign announced Rancho del Oro and pointed me down a street that paralleled the main route. A small shopping plaza strung out on one side of it, Hollywood-western style buildings done in weathered wood with board sidewalks and hitching posts tagged with neatly painted reminders: For Horse Only.

Letters burned into wood announced each business establishment. There was a small grocery and liquor store, a café (named the Feedbag, naturally), a drugstore, and a hay and grain to go with the hitching posts. The offices of Rancho del Oro occupied the corner.

Diagonal parking was marked out opposite the buildings. I left my car and went inside. A tabletop scale model of an elaborate project, complete with little houses from a Monopoly game, dominated the reception area. Since there was only a scattering of houses on the bare hills, I assumed that most of the planning was wishful thinking.

There was nobody at the reception desk by the front door. Two private offices lined the back of the room, glassed from halfway up the interior walls to the ceiling. Claire Ingram sat in one of them studying some papers. She looked up, saw me and waved me inside. The lighting was not kind to her. It brought out brassy highlights in her hair and accented harsh lines and shadows in her face. I added ten years to my estimate of her age.

"That model looks like quite a project," I said. "Do you really expect people to buy this far out?"

"When we started, we had every reason to think so. Interstate 15 is being built. There's lots of room for riding trails. Plenty of people want clean air and open spaces and don't mind a long commute. The gasoline situation changed things, of course. We've had to shift the emphasis of the project, but there are lots of ways to go. Investment, retirement— we're lining up some light industry." Her eyes didn't reflect the enthusiasm in her voice.

I indicated the empty desk out front. "Was that Janet's job?"

"Yes. It's a little slow during the week so I've decided not to replace her with a full-time girl, just somebody on the weekends. We get very busy then."

A map of the project wallpapered one side of the office. From the small number of pins that marked the sold lots, I guessed the weekends weren't busy enough.

"What about Mr. Hunter? Is he joining us?"

"He was feeling pretty rotten. He said to give you his address and have you come by later. But it won't be necessary. Sit down, please. I'm sure I can give you all the information you need."

"Maybe," I said, reserving judgment. "How did you happen to hire Janet?"

"Our accountant, Greg Adams, suggested her.
She was renting a place from his mother. Actually
he made the recommendation to Philip."

"Why not to you?"

"Because he knew I'd never have stood for it.
Philip went over my head."

"You felt that strongly about a stranger?"

"I met her when she first came to Oro. You know
about her and Felix Bak?"

I nodded.

"Well, there was that and besides, I don't think
she ever worked a day in her life. She was hopeless-
ly incompetent."

"Why didn't you fire her?"

"Fat chance. She'd bat those big, sad eyes at
Philip and he'd melt."

"How serious was their relationship?"

"There was nothing between them. Oh, Philip
liked to fantasize, but that's all it was—fantasy . . .
dreams." Her lips curled around the words.

"How well do you know Felix Bak?"

"Well enough." She opened a desk drawer and
dug out a pack of cigarettes and a lighter. "I've
given these damn things up twice. Do you smoke?
No? Good for you." She flicked the lighter and
hungrily drew in smoke.

"Is Bak having any luck selling his paintings?"

My idle question hit a nerve. Even the indoor
lighting couldn't produce that shade of pallor under
her tan. "What paintings?"

"The ones on display at the bank."

"Oh, yes, those. I don't really know. Can we—"

"How about the other things he does?" I asked,
remembering the gas-station attendant's insinua-
tions.

An ugly flush stained her cheeks. "I don't know what you're talking about and I don't have all afternoon to waste on guessing games. Can we get on with this?"

"All right. Tell me about Janet's disappearance."

"Don't make it sound so mysterious. She simply left. Philip insisted on dragging the police into it—the police, can you imagine—and then he wouldn't accept their findings."

"Which were?"

"Janet packed her bags, got in her car and drove away."

Just like before, I thought. A repeat of her old patterns.

Claire must have read something in my face because she said shrewdly, "I'll bet this isn't the first time she's done this, is it? Okay, you don't have to tell me. I know her type."

"And you think you know why she left so abruptly?"

"Yes. I think she got sick of the whole thing with Philip, but she didn't have the guts to tell him so." Claire ground out her cigarette and gave me her full, earnest attention. "Philip won't face the truth, so he comes up with all kinds of bizarre explanations. You're really wasting your time talking to him. Go see Sheriff Bell. He'll confirm what I'm telling you."

It was the logical thing to do, but why did I feel as though I was getting the hard sell? "I plan to talk to the sheriff—"

"Good," she said, relieved. "I knew you'd understand. A few minutes with John Bell and I'm sure you can wrap up your report."

"Not quite. I still want to talk to Philip."

"Didn't you hear a word I said? I thought I explained the situation."

"Oh, you did, but if it's that simple, why are you trying so hard to keep me away from Philip Hunter?"

"Because I want an end to it. Now that Janet's gone, I know Philip will forget in time. I'll see to it. Just leave things alone, Mrs. West, or I'll make it very unpleasant for you around here."

I believed it. Her narrow head and reddish eyes reminded me of a ferret backed into a corner, fighting for its life. Maybe she'd unleashed that feral viciousness on Janet. No wonder Janet had run—if she had run.

Grimly I wondered just how far Claire would go to be rid of the woman who had taken Philip away from her.

4

I WALKED OUT into the blast-furnace midday heat, rearranging the priorities on my list of people to be questioned. If Claire was so set on keeping me away from Philip Hunter, I wanted to know why. It was probably the simplest reason in the world, just what I'd picked up in our conversation: jealousy of Janet. She didn't want him reminded of the girl. Whatever the reason, I put him at the top of my list.

Only one problem. Continuing my run of brilliant detective work, I now had two people I needed to question and no idea how to find either of them. I'd forgotten to ask directions to Bak's and Claire hadn't volunteered Philip's address.

As I waded through the dust that layered the asphalt parking lot, one of my problems solved itself. A lime-green Seville swung into the slot next to mine and Philip got out.

"Mrs. West? I was hoping to catch you here."

If he'd had a shower, you couldn't tell by looking. He wore the same wrinkled shirt under a camel-colored sports coat. His eyes were hidden behind aviator sunglasses.

"Claire said you were too sick to come in," I said.

"I started feeling better after she left, and I really wanted to talk to you. Look, can we get out of this sun? I suppose I could use some more coffee. Shall we?" He waved a hand toward the Feedbag.

I nodded agreement and we walked over to the café.

It tried for cozy and cute. Bags of oats and a bale of hay completed a decorator's imitation of the inside of a barn. Personally, I'd have given a lot at this point for some plain old plastic and chrome. The coffee was good. It came in huge china mugs with real cream and served in a chipped pitcher.

Philip stirred in sugar before he said, "I suppose Claire's been giving you her usual spiel about Janet."

"We talked about it."

"You don't have to be so circumspect." He took off his sunglasses and rubbed the bridge of his nose. His eyes were very dark, almost black, emphasizing the surrounding red-streaked white. "I know Claire thinks I made a damned fool of myself. Look, you'd better know about Claire and me so you'll understand how she feels. We met about ten years ago when we both worked for a big real-estate company in San Bernardino. We had a casual affair that never went very deep and then we drifted apart. I didn't see her for several years. During that time, she got married and divorced. Then, about two years ago, I ran into her again. She had this project lined up. I helped her with the financing and we wound up partners. I think she meant it to be more. Maybe it would have happened eventually, but then I met Janet."

"I guessed it was something like that."

"You can see why Claire reacted the way she did. She wants to believe that Janet left to get away from me and she's convinced the sheriff that's what happened.''

"Is it possible?''

"No, goddammit! I loved Janet. I wanted to marry her. I think we had a good chance. There were problems but we were working them out. For her to just leave without any explanation—no, it's not possible.''

"These problems—do you mind telling me about them?''

"Damn right I mind. Is it really necessary?''

"At this point I don't know what is necessary. But I have to start somewhere. Janet's emotional state seems a good place.''

"Well, if you think it might help. . . .'' He pinched the bridge of his nose again, stared into his cup. "For one thing, I never felt Janet trusted me completely. She didn't want to talk about herself. Not that I cared what happened in the past. I told her that. But she couldn't seem to open up to me. It hurt, but I hoped in time—'' He broke off and waved to the waitress for a refill.

After she left the table, I prompted, "You said, 'for one thing.' Was there more?''

"Yes, and it was my fault. I'm a jealous man, Mrs. West. I couldn't always keep my jealousy under control. I suppose Claire told you about Felix Bak?''

"I already knew about him. Claire said that Janet was renting a house here in town, so I assume Janet had broken off with Bak.''

"She had, but he's got this self-image of a macho lady killer, and he just couldn't accept the fact that Janet left him. He kept hanging around, acting as though they were still involved, although Janet told me it wasn't true. Most of the time I believed her.

But once in a while—God, if I hadn't been so blind with jealousy, I'd have kept that egotistical bastard away from her and this would never have happened.''

"You think he's responsible for Janet's disappearance?''

"I know it. Don't ask me how. All I have is a gut feeling. That wasn't enough to convince the police to put him in a jail cell where he belongs.''

Suddenly the coffee threatened to climb back up in my throat. The man was serious. "Am I reading you right? Do you actually think that Bak *killed* Janet?''

"Damned right I—'' He broke off, looked over my head and said, "Christ! Claire just walked in. Let's get out of here.''

It was a small room. She crossed it before we could slide out of the booth.

"Well, Philip, darling, looks like you've made a miraculous recovery,'' she said with acid sweetness. "Just in time, too. I got hold of the Smiths and they've agreed to talk things over. If you can tear yourself away from Delilah, you can do something constructive like taking care of the office while I'm gone.''

"Sorry, Claire. I can't.''

He threw some dollar bills on the table, brushed past her, took my elbow. I got a glimpse of her face before he steered me out the door. If that look could be scientifically analyzed, it would start a whole new wave of technology in the field of cryogenics.

Philip led the way back into town in his green Seville. "To Janet's place,'' he'd told me in the parking lot. "I'm sure you'll want to see it and we won't be disturbed there.''

I hoped not. I had a lot of questions. Gut feelings are great. I get them myself. But before you talk about murder, you have to come up with one important thing—a body. Until Janet turned up on a coroner's slab, there was still plenty of reason to believe she was simply repeating her old habit of running away. Or so I kept telling myself as I followed Philip past the sheriff's substation.

On the edge of town we turned right down a familiar street. My feeling of déjà vu increased as Philip stopped in front of a house with a browning lawn next door to the one where the blind woman lived. He waved me ahead of him into the eucalyptus-shaded driveway.

We met at the front door. He took out a key and inserted it in the lock. "Janet's rent is paid up till the end of the month. Anyway, Mrs. Adams keeps hoping she'll be back."

So he was close enough to Janet to have a key to her house. As if he were reading my thoughts he held it up. "If you're wondering about this, no, Janet didn't give it to me. I wish I could say she did. But I got it from Mrs. Adams a few days ago."

The house smelled of trapped heat. Our entry stirred up dust that tumbled in the shaft of sunlight from the open door. The living room was starkly plain. White paint on the rough adobe walls had yellowed with age, and wear patterned the beige carpet. A chintz-covered sofa and chair looked comfortable but faded. A coffee table of heavy blond wood sat between them. End tables held chipped lamps.

Philip closed the door, went down a small hallway and flipped on a switch. "Swamp cooler," he explained. A fan whined and cool air trickled through the ducts from the water cooler on top of the house. "It might help a little. Let's sit down, Delilah. Okay if I call you Delilah?"

"Of course, but I'd like to look around."

"Could we talk first? I really ought to get back to the office." He sat down on the sofa, took off his sunglasses and pocketed them, squeezed his hands together. "I know I suggested that we come here, but I didn't realize how painful it would be."

"We'll get through it as quickly as we can." I sat across from him and took a note pad and a ballpoint from my purse. "Before we go back to the subject of Felix Bak, I need some facts for my report."

"Facts," he said bitterly. "What good are facts?"

"Look, I know you're upset. But her father's worried, too." It was a lie, but it sounded good. "If I can take him enough information, maybe he can put some pressure on the police to look for Janet."

"All right. Sorry. We'll do it your way. What do you want to know?"

"Exactly when did Janet disappear?"

"I don't know for sure. Sometime on Thursday night, September fourth. To be more accurate, between five o'clock that night and nine o'clock the following morning."

"Five o'clock is the last time anybody saw her?"

"The last time anybody will admit to seeing her. That's when she left the office. I asked her to go to dinner, but she said she was tired. She just wanted to have a quiet evening and go to bed early. She never came to work the next morning. I called at nine-thirty and every half hour after that until noon. Then I drove here. She was gone."

"Was there any sign of a struggle?"

"No. Everything was just the way it is now. He

must have talked her into going with him someplace
and then—''

''We're back to Felix Bak now.''

''Yes, of course. The man has a violent temper.
Some kids broke into his house last spring. He
caught them and almost killed one of them. He's
been arrested twice for possession of drugs.''

''You can be sure I'll check him out,'' I said. ''Let's
get back to Janet. What happened to her car?''

''Gone,'' he said, his shoulders slumping.

What had Claire said? Janet packed her bags, got
in her car and drove away.

''Go ahead and tell me you think I'm crazy like
the police did,'' he said dully.

''I'm not jumping to conclusions about you or
anybody else at this point. Now, how about any
other people Janet may have been friendly with.
Claire mentioned that your accountant recommended her for the job.''

He nodded. ''Greg Adams. He met Janet through
his mother. She lives next door. Janet rented the
house from her.''

I remembered the older woman sitting with her
face turned toward the sun. ''I think I met her.''

It seemed to startle him. ''When?''

''This morning. I got lost looking for Bak's place.
She was sitting out front. I stopped to ask directions. Of course, I didn't realize she was blind. Or
that Janet lived next door. How well did she know
Janet?''

''Just in passing. Oh, Janet felt sorry for her. She
went out of her way to be kind to the old woman.
Janet was like that. I don't think Emmy can tell you
anything. Still, it might not be a bad idea to talk to
her.''

"I will. Now, how about her son, Greg?"

"What about him? If you think that he and Janet—" He broke off and looked rueful. "Yes, dammit, I was jealous of him, too."

"Did you have reason to be?"

"I don't think so. No. No, of course not. Listen, Delilah, I can't stay here any longer. If you have any more questions, call me later at home. I'll do anything I can, but right now—"

"One thing," I said. "I need directions to Bak's place."

While he traced a map for me on a sheet of my notepaper and added the telephone number, I looked around and asked, "Is this room just the way it was when Janet lived here?"

He followed my gaze. "She didn't decorate, if that's what you mean. She wasn't here long enough."

"Then why did you get the key from Mrs. Adams?"

"What?"

"There are no plants to water. No cats to feed. Why come here?"

"I don't know. I just thought being here would help, but I was wrong." He handed it to me. "Do me a favor. Lock up when you leave, then give the key to Emmy, will you? I don't think I can stand to come here again. And please, call me if you find out anything."

I agreed and watched him stride across the drying grass to his car. Then I closed the door and turned back to the silent room. It still seemed funny that Janet had lived here all those weeks and not made one mark on her surroundings. No plants or pictures to decorate the living room. The kitchen had a small table bracketed by two chairs, but not even a salt shaker sat on top. Pink-tiled counters were also bare. The cupboards held only a few staples. A carton of yogurt and half of a moldy cantaloupe were the only things in the refrigerator.

The bathroom was clean and empty, the bedroom impersonally neat. A plain chenille spread covered the bed. Nothing under it except dust. A few wire coat hangers occupied the closet. I felt around on the shelves but only found more dust. The dresser yielded the only thing that Janet had left behind: a broken tortoiseshell comb.

Regardless of what Philip thought, it looked to me as though she'd used this place like a motel room. Just another place to leave behind.

There was nothing here to tell me where she'd gone. I picked up my purse, turned off the cooler and let myself out the front door, locking it behind me. I looked at my watch. Four-thirty. The sun angled through the eucalyptus in slashes of yellow light. Depending on how long it took to talk to Emmy Adams, there might still be time to go find Bak before dark.

I walked across the lawn toward the house that was a duplicate of the one Janet lived in. The grass made dry crackling sounds under my feet. It needed water badly. Who took care of it, I wondered. You'd think Mrs. Adams's son would see the shape the lawn was in when he visited his mother.

If he visits his mother, I thought as I climbed up the narrow front stoop and rang the bell. Greg Adams was still an unknown quantity. All I knew about him was the fact that he recommended Janet for the job with Claire and Philip.

Nobody answered the door so I rang again and

knocked. No response. I tried to ignore the uneasy movement in my stomach. She's out, I told myself. Dammit, you don't even know the woman and you certainly don't know her schedule. The son does visit and he took his mother shopping or to dinner.

I headed for my car. I'd go see Felix Bak and stop on the way back to drop off the key and talk to Mrs. Adams. I reached for the car door, hesitated. It was only four-thirty. Her son wouldn't be through with work yet.

Silly, I thought. So he took off early.

It made perfect sense, but I released the door handle and walked back to the house. I pounded and called, "Mrs. Adams, are you in there? Are you all right?"

No answer. I went around to the back and hammered on the door. There was a window in it but it was curtained and I couldn't see inside. I rattled the knob but the door was locked. The apprehension had grown to an icy hollowness in the middle of my chest.

There was a window a few feet over. I pushed through a thorny sprawl of pyracantha bushes and looked into the kitchen through the bottom pane. The window was over a sink. To the left I could see a stretch of pink-tiled counter, a stove top. A tea-kettle sat on the stove. Next to it on the counter was a mug with the tag of a tea bag hanging over the side.

A refrigerator gleamed whitely in one corner. In the other stood a small table and a chair. One chair. It was exactly like the set in the house next door and there should have been two of them. Why wasn't the other one there? Blind people keep everything in its proper place.

I was shivering now in the hot dry air. I couldn't see the floor. I wasn't tall enough. I searched the ground for something to stand on, found nothing. But I did notice a crack in the adobe wall about a foot from the ground. I put my toe in it, grabbed a window ledge and pulled myself up.

I could see the second chair. Tipped over on its side. The ice in my chest spread outward into my bloodstream.

Only a portion of the floor was visible but it was enough. I saw legs, the hem of a print dress. Enough to know that Emmy Adams lay limp and still between the overturned chair and the back door.

5

I RAN TO THE BACK DOOR and beat the edge of my purse against the lower square of window until it shattered. A heavy smell of gas billowed out. Ignoring the jagged remnants, I reached inside, turned the lock and threw open the door.

A choking wave of gas hit me. Trying not to breathe, I rushed in and slid my hands under Mrs. Adams's shoulders, but she was too heavy to lift. I grabbed her wrists, swinging her arms over her head and pulled. My lungs were bursting by the time I dragged her heavy body out the door. I gulped some clean air, clamped my hand over my nose and mouth and dashed back inside the kitchen.

My eyes fought the stinging fumes with a flood of tears. I could barely see the stove, but I heard the deadly hiss as I found the knobs and turned off the front and back burners.

I stumbled outside. A spasm of coughing shook me. I fought it as I fell to my knees beside Mrs. Adams. Her skin was pasty gray; her eyes closed. She wasn't breathing. I fumbled with her wrist, felt a pulse—faint, but it was there.

Thank God, thank God, I kept repeating over and over in my mind. My face was wet as I lifted her chin and pinched her nose shut. Ignoring my revulsion and my own body's demands for rest, for oxygen, I pushed air into her lungs.

Inhale. Exhale. Again and again.

Breathe, I pleaded silently. Breathe.

No response. I rammed my finger inside her mouth, seeking an obstacle to the airway. Hard teeth, soft tissue, spittle—but no blockage.

Start the procedure again. In. Out. My lungs burned with the effort but it wasn't doing any good.

Help, I thought. I have to get help.

I left her there and ran inside. The gas had cleared a little but the residue stung my eyes and burned my bronchial tubes. No phone in the kitchen. I stumbled through the house, finally found it beside the bed. My fingers felt thick and useless as I dialed, my throat raw as I croaked out a plea to the operator. She promised to send help and I ran back to Mrs. Adams.

"They're coming," I said, dropping down beside the still form. "You'll be all right."

I yanked her head back, pressed my mouth over hers. Her lips felt cool, too cool.

No, I thought fiercely and blew air in sharp, forceful puffs.

But she was so still. The pulse had beat with only the weakest flicker of life. Maybe it hadn't beat at all. Maybe I imagined it.

I reached for her wrist. Nothing. I moved my fingertips to the inner elbow, her throat, searching for a feeble throb. Nothing. For an instant I was thrust back in time. Blackness. Cold rain on my face. Jack's body in my arms, his life bleeding away and nothing, nothing I could do.

No. Not this time. The thought was like a scream inside my head.

I clasped my hands on her chest, began the rhythm of C.P.R. Push, count, breathe. I shut out the clamoring fears and concentrated everything on the routine. Dimly I heard a siren, voices. Then strong hands pulled me away.

"We'll take over now," somebody said.

His face was a blur, but I saw his uniform and other uniformed men behind him before the darkness closed in.

I AWAKENED to the hard press of an oxygen mask clamped over my nose and mouth. I was lying on the ground. A fireman knelt beside me. "Okay now?" he asked.

Over his shoulder I could see the paramedics picking up a stretcher. One held an I.V. bottle, light glinting off the glass container.

At least the sun's out, I thought. She likes sunlight on her face. I pulled the mask off and sat up as they rushed away.

"Better take it easy," the fireman cautioned. "We'll get you to the hospital."

"It's not necessary. I'm all right now. How's Mrs. Adams?"

"It doesn't look good, but they'll do what they can."

"I should have called you first," I said. "I should have started C.P.R. sooner."

"Don't blame yourself. You did the best you could. If she's got any chance at all, it's because of you."

Another fireman came over, dropped down on one knee beside us, took off his hat. "The house seems to be pretty clear now. We can't find any leaks."

"It was the stove," I said. "I shut it off."

"Figured that." He wiped his forehead with his sleeve. "The pilot light was out. She must have turned on the burner for some tea and then forgot it. Damned lucky thing the water heater and the furnace were in the garage. The place could have blown sky-high. Poor old Mrs. Adams. She always seemed to manage so well. I'd better call Greg and tell him what happened."

A paging device clipped to his belt beeped a warning. "Damn," he said. "What now?"

A fireman ran around the house calling, "Chief? Brush fire north of town."

"We've got to roll," the fire chief said. "Please, miss. Call Greg for me."

There wasn't time to tell him I didn't know Greg Adams, didn't know where to reach him. They raced to the truck and roared off, sirens screaming.

I stood up slowly, brushing bits of dry grass from my clothes. It still hurt to breathe and my legs were as mushy as overcooked zucchini. I didn't want to go back in that house, but I had to make the call. Anyway, my purse was gone. I must have dropped it when I dragged Mrs. Adams outside.

The back door stood open. A faint, cloying smell lingered, starting a wave of nausea as I entered the kitchen. Glass from the broken window crunched beneath my feet. My purse lay under the table. I reached for it and something caught my eye, a dull gleam of metal along the wall. I picked it out of the glass shards.

A necklace. Slender gold chain with a pendant etched with a stylized design of fish. I remembered it hanging around Mrs. Adams's neck, catching the sun.

The chain was broken. It must have caught beneath her body as I dragged her out the door. I took it with me into the bedroom, let the metallic links slide from my hand to the bedside table as I picked up the telephone and dialed information.

There was no listing for his residence, but there was one for Greg Adams, C.P.A. A woman answered in businesslike tones. He wasn't in, she told me. The hospital had already called. I thanked her and hung up. I thought about checking on Mrs. Adams but I couldn't do it. I was afraid of what I would find out.

"There *was* a pulse," I whispered, knotting my hands into fists and pounding on my knees. "I felt it."

She was alive. She had to be. But the stench of death was on my clothes, in my nostrils. Vomit rose in my throat. I stumbled to the bathroom and crouched over the toilet until my stomach was empty. Then I splashed cold water on my face and went back to sit on the bed.

The dizziness passed and I became aware of my surroundings. The layout was identical to Janet's rented house. Even the furniture was similar. But this room seemed warm and lived-in. The bed was covered with a quilted comforter, soft to the touch. Plants filled the top of an old chest placed under a window. Books, printed in Braille, lay on the nightstand.

I got up and walked around the room. A terrycloth robe hung in the bathroom. Shoes stood in a precise row in the closet. The top of her dresser held a hairbrush, a shoe horn, a pile of envelopes.

Who writes to a blind woman, I wondered.

Pacific Telephone Company, read the return address of the one on top. Bills, then. Unopened. I went back and sat on the bed beside the nightstand, stared at the telephone. I ought to call the hospital. No, it was too soon. All I'd get was some standard officious brush-off.

I reached out and touched the stack of books on the table. Maybe she'd be able to read again soon, to finish the book she had started. Something marked her place in it. A large square of stiff paper.

Drawn by curiosity, I pulled it out. It was a greeting card. Beneath an embossed outline of a rose, raised letters wished Happy Birthday. The message inside was unreadable because it was in Braille. There was a signature. The elegant script read, "Love, Jannie."

"Jannie" was Janet Valek.

Philip had said that Janet went out of her way to be kind to Emmy Adams. His words indicated a one-way relationship. But it must have gone deeper than that if the older woman gave her an affectionate nickname.

Feeling guilty, I slipped the card back in place. I had no right to pry, but it was an occupational disease like fallen arches or black lung.

I went back to the telephone, tapped a fingernail against the hard plastic. I picked up the necklace, fingering the gold pendant. There was no need for me to stay here any longer. Her son had been notified and I had my own job to do. I'd call the hospital later after she was stabilized. Maybe she'd be able to talk to me then.

I picked up my purse and headed for the kitchen, wondering what I should do about closing up the house. Surely it was safe now, but I couldn't go away and leave it open. Maybe I should sweep up

the glass, do something about the broken pane.
There was a broom closet in the kitchen. The necklace was still in my hand. Absently, I slipped it into
my pocket as I took out a dustpan and a long-
handled brush.

It was getting dark in the room. I flipped on the
light and began cleaning up. I was down on my
knees searching for elusive splinters, when I heard
a key in the lock and the front door swinging open.
Quick firm steps sounded on the tile entry. By the
time I got to my feet a man came into the kitchen
and stood there, framed in the arch of the doorway.

He was medium height, about my age, with hard-
muscled shoulders and lean hips. Thick ash blond
hair topped a deeply tanned face. His dress shirt
was unbuttoned at the collar, the knot in his tie
pulled open. He looked like he'd be a lot more comfortable in jeans.

"I'm Greg Adams." His voice was harsh, his gray
eyes full of cold shadows. "I want to know what
happened here."

"She was making tea," I said, chilled by the grim
set of his jaw. "The pilot light was out."

"I just talked to her on the phone at lunchtime.
She was fine. How the hell—" He broke off, staring
at me as if he saw me for the first time. "Sorry. I
didn't mean to jump on you. They told me at the
hospital that a woman dragged my mother from the
house. You?"

I nodded.

"They didn't know your name," he said.

"Delilah West." I realized the dustpan was still in
my hand. I put it down on the table and said awkwardly. "I thought I'd clean up before I left. There
was broken glass and I didn't want your mother—"

I stopped. My tongue felt large and unwieldy. "She is. . . all right?"

The shadows deepened in his eyes and he shook his head in a gesture of finality.

"But she was alive," I said numbly. "They had an I.V. going." In my mind I saw the stretcher and the sun glinting off the bottle.

"I live in a dark world," she had told me. "Sometimes I just have to feel the sun on my face."

Now there would be no more sunlight, only cold uncaring darkness. I had been the only person who could have saved her. If I'd come earlier, hadn't wasted time deciding something was wrong—a cry started deep inside my soul, a cry of grief and rage that seared every nerve ending in my body. I clamped my jaws shut and it came out as a moan. My legs trembled violently and I swayed forward.

Greg crossed the small room and grabbed me. I leaned against him, feeling his strength flow like a current between us. Quickly I pulled away, mumbling, "I'm okay," but I had to clutch the table for support.

"You'd better sit down," he said, guiding me into a chair. Then he went to a cupboard, took out a bottle of Scotch and two glasses. "Here. You look like you need this."

I gulped the liquor gratefully. "Sorry," I said. "You've got enough to handle right now. Ordinarily I don't come unglued like that. I've seen death before, but somehow I never get used to it, and God, how I hate it. It makes me feel so damned helpless."

"I thought your name sounded familiar," he said. "You're the private detective who's looking for Janet."

"Word travels fast." I took another swallow and shuddered, welcoming the fiery spasm the Scotch created in my throat and stomach.

"Is that how you happened to be here at my mother's?" he asked.

"Yes. I came over to talk to her about Janet."

"Who's your client? Did Philip Hunter hire you to look for her?"

"No," I said. "Her father did. Actually he knew she was in Oro. But they hadn't heard from her and her brother's worried. I came to check on things and found out she'd disappeared."

"You may not be working for Philip, but I'll bet you've talked to him. As far as I know, he's the only one who subscribes to that disappearance theory."

"You don't?"

"No, and frankly, Miss—" he looked down at my ring finger "—*Mrs*. West, I've got too much on my mind right now to think about it."

"Of course," I said, but the thought crossed my mind that he certainly wasn't showing much grief. I'd reacted as if Emmy's death was an intensely personal loss but he seemed completely in control. "I wish there had been something else I could have done."

"You did everything you could. I haven't thanked you for trying to save Emmy's life."

His eyes changed color. They'd been gray before, forbidding, stormy. Now they warmed to green, like the sun shining through an ocean wave.

"It wasn't enough," I said.

"Don't think that way. The paramedics told me you did everything possible. I thank you for that."

He drained his Scotch, got up and took his glass to the sink. The cup with its unused tea bag still sat on the counter. He reached out to touch it and the look on his face told me I'd been wrong about his grief. He was simply keeping it all inside.

"People told me I was crazy to let her live here alone. But she wanted it that way. I worried about falls, fires, but a goddamn stupid cup of tea...."

I had a sudden memory of the way Mrs. Adams's head turned at the sound of my feet on the graveled edge of the asphalt driveway when I approached her this morning.

"You mother had good hearing," I said.

"What?"

"Gas makes a hissing sound. I wonder why she didn't hear it?"

I'd heard it when I staggered inside. I remembered the feel of the plastic knobs as I shut off the gas under the teakettle and the sound....

"I suppose we'll never really know what happened," he said.

"That depends on the answer to one more question. Mr. Adams, do you know anybody who wanted to see your mother dead?"

6

GREG ADAMS TURNED ON ME, his eyes cold with fury. "What the hell are you talking about? If this is some kind of a sick joke—"

"I wouldn't joke about something like this," I said. "Please listen to me for a minute. I think there's a strong possibility that your mother's death was not an accident."

"You already have a case, Mrs. West. Is it really necessary to drum up business like this?"

The bitterness in his voice stung. He must have seen the pain in my face, because he sat down again and said, "Christ, that was rotten of me. I'm sorry. Look, what reason could you possibly have for saying something like that?"

"Because when I came in here to shut off the gas, there were two burners turned on. Not just the one under the teakettle. The back one, too."

He shook his head. "Maybe I'm dense or maybe I'm not tracking right now, but I don't see what you're driving at."

"Let me ask you a couple of questions," I said. "Why would your mother turn on two burners to boil one kettle of water? And why didn't she hear the sound the gas made when it failed to light?"

"Something distracted her. She lost track of what

she was doing. I don't know. After all, she was blind."

"But not deaf and certainly not stupid. Look, you could be right," I said. "But what if she was already groggy from the gas when she came out to make her tea because somebody else had turned on that back burner?"

"That's crazy," he said angrily. "Emmy didn't have many friends, but she certainly didn't have any enemies. It's bad enough that she's dead, but for you to suggest that somebody deliberately—no, I don't believe it." He stood up, his tone changing to one of dismissal. "Now, you'll have to excuse me. I've got a lot of things to do."

IT WAS SEVEN-THIRTY when I found the Old Prospector's Motel in a grove of acacia and pepper trees on the edge of town. Alternating red and yellow neon promised color TV, queen-size beds and a café. A western-style false front tried for a slick, modern look, but the old cinder block construction gave away the building's age. Inside the office business wasn't exactly booming, but at least half the keys were gone from the pegboard holder. I wondered how much gold the owner would find when the Interstate was completed and the big boys like Holiday Inn and Motel Six moved in.

I signed the register and tilted my head in the direction of the café. "How late are they open?" I asked.

"Eleven o'clock. Best food in town," the manager assured me.

I trudged over to find out. I really needed a shower and a change of clothes, but I was afraid once I got inside the motel room I'd go straight to bed. I felt hollow and weak and I knew I should put some food in my stomach.

It only took one bite of hamburger to tell me that the manager exaggerated a lot. It was greasy and tasteless but I chewed solidly, washing it down with a glass of milk.

"How about dessert?" the waitress asked with a brightly lacquered smile.

I decided not to risk it, paid my check and started for my room. Halfway there my stomach put out warning signals and I barely made it inside before it rebelled completely. So much for supper. I wrung out a towel under the cold tap, lay down on the bed and draped it across my forehead. While I waited for the room to stop spinning, I thought about the aftereffects of gas fumes and wondered if I would die if I didn't go to the hospital.

When I decided I was going to live, I rolled over and picked up the telephone, asked the office for an outside line and dialed.

"Rita? It's Delilah. Any messages?"

"Just a dozen or so from a client. David Valek. Remember him?"

"I didn't forget, Rita."

"You could've fooled me," she said. "How's Janet?"

I stared at a water blotch on the ceiling. "I don't know. I didn't talk to her yet. There are complications. Nothing to do with Janet. I'll explain tomorrow. Tell David I'll have some news soon."

Hanging up is the only way to turn Rita off, so I hung up. I needed a shower, but I was afraid I might fall down and drown, so I took off my clothes, dropped them on the floor and went to bed.

The pillows were too soft and the mattress was

too hard, but I was too tired to care. Red and yellow fingers of light pulsed through the skimpy curtains. I pulled the sheet over my head. It shut out the neon flashes, but it wasn't so easy to stop the little needle of doubt busily stitching up a patchwork of questions in my head.

I'd told Rita that the complications I'd run into in Oro had nothing to do with Janet. It wasn't true. Janet was gone and a woman who was close to her was dead. I couldn't help but wonder if there was a connection.

I WOKE UP TO SUNLIGHT and a bird doing a solo performance just outside my window. The song started out sweet and melodious, a trilling four-note run that ended on the most god-awful squawk imaginable. I tried to go back to sleep but it was useless. One thing about that bird. He was no quitter. He was determined to do it until he got it right.

By the time I convinced myself to get up, shower and dress, the café was open for business. Cautiously I tried Rice Krispies and skim milk. When that stayed down, I ordered coffee. It was black and bitter, but it did the things that coffee was supposed to do, so I had a second cup while I read the paper.

Emmy Adams's death got about one inch of type in the Riverside County section of the L.A. *Times*. In the article she became a tragic victim and I was the unidentified passerby who tried to save her.

The incident rated a headline in the weekly issue of the Oro *Gazette*: Local Woman Dead of Gas Poisoning. The accompanying article was brief with a factual but hurried tone as if the reporter was trying to beat a deadline. It told me that Emmy was sixty-two years old and a long-time resident of Oro.

That was all except for a sidebar about the dangers of home accidents.

"Big help," I muttered, threw the paper in the trash and drove out to the sheriff's substation.

It was a plain one-story rectangle, painted the color of the sandy earth in the surrounding countryside. Scraggly junipers and ice plant struggled for survival in a narrow strip by the front door, the tips of the evergreen needles dry and brown and the fleshy leaves of the succulent ground cover shriveling from the long summer drought.

A harried young officer in summer tans and a regulation mustache took my name and buzzed John Bell. While I waited, I studied a large poster on the bulletin board that showed a cop and Mr. Average Citizen clasping hands above a legend that proclaimed, "Pardners in Keeping the Peace."

"The sheriff can give you a few minutes," the policeman said, pointing out an office down the hall. "But you'll have to make it brief. We're getting ready for an open house this afternoon."

That explained the poster, I thought, as I went to tap on Bell's door.

I got a gruff, "Come."

Bell was a gently balding man with sloping shoulders, metal-rimmed glasses and sun wrinkles radiating from mild blue eyes. He didn't stand up and he offered me his hand across a desk that overflowed with paperwork.

"Ms. West," he said. "Sit down, please. I heard you were in town. What can I do for you?"

Somebody had told him about me. Claire Ingram? Maybe not. He certainly seemed cordial enough.

"As you probably know, I'm looking for Janet Valek," I said, settling into the chair across from

him and handing him my card. "Her father retained
me to check up on her, but when I arrived in Oro I
found she's been missing for three weeks. Would
you mind filling me in on the case?"

"Be happy to, but as far as I know there is no
'case,' Ms. West. The girl just packed up one day
and left."

"Philip Hunter doesn't think it happened that
way."

"I know and, frankly, he's been making a real
nuisance of himself about it."

"You didn't think his fears justified some sort of
investigation? Seems to me it would have been simple enough to trace her car, perhaps check with her
family to see if she was all right."

"Sure, I could've done that. I could check out
every girl friend or boyfriend who get their noses
out of joint and run away. But I've got a limited
staff here and a big chunk of the county to patrol.
During the past three weeks we've had a rash of
armed robberies, the usual assortment of domestic
fights and a murder. Compared to that a thirty-two-
year-old woman who left of her own volition gets
pretty low priority."

He stood up and came around the desk with his
hand out. "Nice meeting you, Ms. West. Sorry this
turned into a wild-goose chase for you. Next time
you're in Oro, be sure to drop in."

I didn't take his hand and he dropped it, the
pleasant smile gone.

"I understand your feelings about Janet's disappearance," I said. "I felt pretty much the same way
until Emmy Adams was killed yesterday."

"Killed?" He stared at me. "Where?"

"Here in Oro."

"The only death I know about was the old lady who died from gas poisoning. What do you know about it?"

"I was the one who dragged her from the house. She lived next door to Janet. As a matter of fact, she was Janet's landlady and they were friends."

He went back to his chair and gave me his full attention. "Are you saying she didn't die from the gas?"

"No. I don't think there's any doubt about that." I summarized what I'd found in Mrs. Adams's kitchen the day before. He listened carefully, but I could see the skepticism growing in his eyes.

"Seems pretty thin to me," he said when I finished. "The woman was blind. She was getting old. It can easily be explained. As far as that goes, Ms. West, you were under a lot of stress yourself. Somebody's life was in your hands. Then, too, you probably had a good dose of gas. Really, what do we have except your memory of that incident?"

"You think I imagined it?"

"I believe you made a mistake. Hell, it's completely understandable under the circumstances. Maybe you turned on that other burner while you were fumbling around. At any rate, I don't think it was anything but a tragic accident."

The telephone rang. He answered, snapped a terse reply and hung up. "Sorry, Ms. West, but things are piling up on me. In addition to everything else we've got our annual open house today." He didn't sound as though it was his favorite happening.

"I'm going to do some more checking," I said. "I still have to find Janet Valek."

"Go right ahead. I'm assuming you know the

boundaries, Ms. West. Don't step over and we'll get along just fine.''

The pleasant voice had a definite edge, and the mild blue eyes were hard behind the glasses. Steel under velvet, I thought. Much nicer than Claire Ingram's warning but the message was the same: Do your little job, Delilah, and then get the hell out of town.

I turned a deaf ear and went to finish what I came to do in the first place.

This time I found Mesquite Canyon.

7

A SMALL WOODEN SIGN marked with an artist's palette and the name Bak pointed the way up a wrinkle in the hills. I bounced along two potholed ruts that followed the course of a dry stream bed for about two hundred yards before they gave up and quit. Off to the left, a small house backed up against a rocky wall. It was made of rough-sawn lumber, weathered to silver, and looked as though the builder had slapped it together out of leftovers before abandoning it as hopeless.

Trapped heat raised the temperature by at least ten degrees. The vegetation clinging to the canyon walls was gray white, like drying bones. Along the margin of the creek bed, mesquite bushes provided the only touch of green. A hot breeze ruffled long flat pods that hung in clusters among feathery-leafed branches.

In front of the house, a battered Ranchero gathered dust. I parked next to it, got out and took about three steps before a piece of the pickup's shadow detached itself and materialized into a large dog with burr-clotted fur. I froze as he stood there, watching me. A growl began low in his throat and ended in a bark that rattled off the surrounding sandstone.

From inside the house a male voice bellowed, "Shut up, you damned mutt!"

The directive didn't impress the dog; he barked again. I stood still and gauged the distance back to my car, but his tail gave a couple of haphazard wags and he looked like it was too much trouble to bite me.

I said, "Nice doggie," just in case.

He yawned, lifted his leg against my rear tire and lay back down in the dusty shadows. A small lizard scurried between us, but that stirred up less interest than I did. I left him to catch up on his sleep, walked over to the house and went up three rotten steps to cross the porch and knock.

The door flew open with a groan of rusty hinges and a man snarled, "What the hell is it?"

He was naked except for a pair of red and white striped boxer shorts. Curly black hair covered his head and most of his chest. Dark stubble shadowed a long jaw. Bushy eyebrows joined together in a scowl that softened as he stared at me, blinked and then looked me up and down with a smile.

"Well, well," he said. "I'll have to apologize to the mutt. This time I'm glad he woke me up."

Before he could get too enthusiatic, I said, "I'm a private detective. I'm looking for Janet Valek."

"Christ," he said in disgust. "Hunter really has got a hair across his ass. Go away and let me go back to sleep."

"I'm not working for Philip Hunter," I said. "Janet's father sent me. Look, I've had a long hot drive. All I want to do is ask you a couple of questions."

"Well...." He did another inventory and shrugged. "Why not? Come on in while I get dressed."

I followed him in warily, estimating the distance back to the door.

If the outside of the house was bad, the inside was a total disaster. Lumpy furniture sagged against peeling walls. Clothing layered the floor along with newspapers, beer cans and other debris that didn't invite a closer inspection. Paintings hung on every available inch of wall space, a violent conflagration of color that guaranteed to give you a migraine in five minutes flat.

The kitchen took up about three square feet in one corner. I didn't want to know about the bathroom.

By contrast the room beyond was a miracle of order. Through an open doorway I could see an easel, the corner of a worktable that held a quart fruit jar full of brushes, rows of paint tubes, cleaning cloths. More paintings lined the walls above a row of low cupboards.

Bak poked around on the floor, came up with a pair of khaki shorts and a blue tank top. "You see my razor anywhere?" he asked.

I picked it out of a litter of dirty paper plates on the coffee table and he buzzed it over his whiskers while he took a six-pack of Coors from a small refrigerator. He brought the beer over, shoveled off a space on the couch for us with a wave of his hand.

"Sit down," he said, offering one of the cans.

Before I'd swallowed five times Bak had finished his, tossed the can on the floor and peeled the pull tab from a second.

"Damn country dries you out," he remarked, moving an inch closer to examine the V-neck opening of my blouse. "What did you say your name was?"

"I didn't, but it's Delilah West."

"Delilah. Sexy name. I like it." Circles of sweat already stained the tank top and the shave had left uneven patches of stubble.

"Thanks," I said. "About Janet. How long did she stay here with you?"

"About two weeks. Then she moved into town."

"I know. She rented a place from Mrs. Adams."

"You talked to Emmy?"

"I tried to. Maybe you haven't heard yet, Mr. Bak. Emmy Adams is dead." I watched him closely, but his surprise seemed genuine.

"Dead? No, I didn't hear about it. Funny Greg didn't stop by and tell me. He's got a place a couple of miles out. What was it? Her heart?"

"No," I said. "The pilot light was off on her kitchen stove. Somehow the gas was left on. Are the Adamses friends of yours?"

"Not really. I rent this place from them."

"Did you introduce Janet to them?"

He thought about it, shook his head. "Damned if I know. I must have."

"Why did she leave here, Mr. Bak?"

"Felix. It's Felix, and if Hunter's been giving you that bullshit about her dropping me cold, forget it. She just didn't like roughing it, that's all. We stayed friends." He gave me a smile that just missed being a leer. "Good friends."

Impossible to picture the elegant woman I'd met that day in Forty Carrots living here in this squalor with Felix, to imagine an intimate relationship between the two of them.

"I thought when she moved into town she started seeing Philip Hunter," I said.

"She did. So what? I didn't have exclusives."

"If you were such good friends, why didn't Janet tell you where she was going?"

"Hey, it's a free country. Janet doesn't report to me. Matter of fact, I don't know if I like her old man trying to keep tabs on her. Why don't we forget about Janet and talk about something interesting?"

He flashed another wolfish grin and put his hand on my bare knee, began moving it up my thigh.

"Maybe later," I said, removing his hand and smiling back with what I hoped he would take for provocative promise. "As far as Janet's concerned, I agree with you. She's old enough to do what she likes. But her younger brother is kind of worried about her. I'm just trying to make sure she's okay. You could really help me out if you answer a few more questions."

"Fire away."

Maybe my smile promised more than I intended. He moved closer and slid a hairy arm along the back of the couch.

"How long have you known Janet?" I asked.

"I met her in June over in Laguna Beach. I really thought she was something. Funny thing, I didn't think she dug me quite as much. Goes to show how wrong you can be. About two weeks after I came back, there she was on my doorstep. Just like you."

His fingers curled around my neck, worked their way inside the neck of my blouse and began sliding my bra strap off my shoulder. He smelled of beer, stale sweat and unbrushed teeth. Quickly I drained my beer and held out the can.

"How about a refill?" I asked.

He looked annoyed but he backed off long enough to reach for another can. I took advantage of the opening to jump up and pretend a fascination with his paintings.

"These are really—" I searched for a word and came up with, "extraordinary."

He brought my beer over and stood there, head tipped back, to stare at them broodingly. "Yeah. Just wish the critics thought so. I hoped to get a place in one of the art shows at the festival in Laguna but—" He crumpled his beer can and hurled it into a corner. "The hell with it. How'd you like to see some of my other stuff? I did one of Janet you might be interested in."

He gestured toward the studio.

And come into my parlor, I thought as I followed him inside. Was this going to be his private collection that I kept hearing about?

A large cupboard stood in one corner of the room. The door could be secured by a sturdy padlock, but at the moment the lock hung open on the hasp. He extracted a large canvas, brought it over and set it on the easel.

The painting hit me like a physical blow. A porno picture is graphic, but the realism is two-dimensional. Bak's paint and brushes probed beneath skin and body hair, subtly evoking a totally corrupt sexuality. It was definitely Janet Valek, but nothing was left of the woman I'd met except a superficial physical rendering.

Was this the real Janet? The strange kinship I'd felt for her vanished, and I wondered what made me think I'd ever known this woman at all. My stomach crawled with revulsion and I turned away, ready to bolt from the room, but I stumbled against Felix.

"How about it?" he murmured, moving his hands

over my body. "The one I do of you will be like your name. Delilah. Just a touch of biblical overtones. Sodom and Gomorrah—oh, yeah!"

"Hey, slow down." I resisted the urge to bring my knee up into his crotch and run. I even managed a weak laugh as I wriggled from his grasp. "I don't like to rush into things. Anyway, I told you I've got a job to finish. After that, well, who knows?"

I lifted my beer can in a toast and made a fast exit into the other room.

"I told you all I know," he said, following me, his face dark with sullen truculence.

I couldn't afford to lose him now. I sat down on the couch and crossed my legs, letting my skirt inch up above my knees. "Just a couple more questions, okay? Tell me about Janet and Philip Hunter. He says he was serious about her. Was it mutual?"

"Nah. She was just stringing him along," he said, joining me on the couch. "As for Philip, hell, Janet smells like money to me and Philip's got a keener nose than I have. Could be that real-estate business of his is going under and he was looking for an out."

"You do know he thinks you had something to do with Janet's disappearance?"

"Oh, yeah. He had the cops out here a couple of days after she left. Wanted them to start digging up the canyon. Can you believe that? Guy's a first-class asshole. I can see him getting worried about her, but Christ—" He shook his head.

"Claire Ingram thinks that Janet left to get away from him."

"Good ole Claire," he said with a smirk. "She does like to hang on. It takes a special man to keep Claire in her place. Philip just doesn't have what it takes."

"You think she could be right about Janet?" I persisted. "Did Janet say anything to you about it?"

"No. I didn't see her for a few days before she left. I was working. When I'm into a painting, I lose track of things. I think we were supposed to have dinner." He stopped, his eyes fixed and far away for a moment before he blinked and went on. "Yeah, dinner. Anyway, I was pretty high. The painting does that to me. And I'd smoked a lot of dope. I had some real good Colombian...and I killed off a few bottles of wine. I was supposed to go up to Riverside to see somebody about an exhibit so I took off. I guess I forgot all about Janet."

He was getting restless. He patted my knee but it was a routine caress, more like a doctor testing for a reflex. "Sorry, I can't help you, Delilah. But listen," he said, standing up. "Maybe we can get together real soon when you're not so busy."

He steered me outside and practically shut the door in my face.

What was that all about, I wondered as I walked slowly toward my car.

By the time I got back to town, I was sure I knew.

8

THE INTERVIEW WITH BAK left me feeling as though I'd taken a stroll in a cow pasture and hadn't watched my step. I drove back to my motel and took a steaming shower in a futile effort to wash away the filth. The hot water ran out before I felt clean so I had to rinse off under the cold. Shivering, I slipped on my bathrobe and sat on the bed to towel dry my hair and put the case into some kind of order.

Janet had left Oro three weeks ago. That was the only hard fact I had. Everything else was a blur of half-truths and confusion. But I was sure I knew why Felix had rushed me out of the house. He'd pulled something from the murky slime of his memory. I wished to hell I knew what it was.

Maybe he had talked to Janet that night she disappeared. Maybe she told him where she was going. All I could hope was that he'd get in touch with her and tell her about me. That she'd call David and the case would be over. I could go back to the blessed routine of insurance investigations and personnel checks.

I indulged in the fantasy for a couple of minutes before I grimly put it aside. Too easy. Anyway, it was no longer a case of Janet simply leaving town. A woman was dead.

A memory of Emmy Adams overpowered me like the rotting fish odor of the gas that took her life. My breath came in shallow gasps and my heart pounded. I could feel her cool lips, the flaccid pulseless wrists, the solid resistance of her body as I fought to give it life.

Stop it, I told myself, tearing my thoughts away, but I remembered every detail. And no matter what Sheriff Bell said there had been two burners wide open on that stove, pouring their noxious fumes into the house.

What if it really was murder? I shivered. It was true I didn't know the woman. Her background could've produced any number of enemies. It was the coincidence that bothered me. I arrived in Oro and before I got to Emmy, she was killed. That pointed to one conclusion—she knew something about Janet's disappearance that somebody didn't want me to find out.

But what? The two were friends, close enough for Janet to give the older woman a special birthday card. Close enough for Janet to confide in her?

Damn it, I thought. This is getting me nowhere.

I got up and paced the floor. The maid hadn't come in yet. The clothes I'd worn the day before still lay in a crumpled heap where I'd dropped them when I'd stumbled into bed. I picked up the dress, shook it out, folded it. Something fell from the pocket and slithered into a little gold mound on the floor.

Emmy's necklace. I picked it up and sat back down on the edge of the bed to stare at it. What in the world was it doing in the pocket of my dress? Vaguely, I remembered putting it there before I swept up the glass from her kitchen floor. Greg's arrival made me forget it.

I'll have to return it, I thought, rubbing my fingers over the pendant.

It was beautifully made. Heavy gold. A raised design of a stylized fish.

Pisces, I thought suddenly, recognizing the astrological symbol.

Little twinges of excitement pulsed in my brain. I don't know the zodiac signs that well. I seemed to remember Cancer for July and Leo for August, but what the hell was Pisces?

I looked around for a newspaper, but there was no printed matter in the room except a local telephone directory and a Gideon Bible. I did some fast thinking and looked up Greg's office number. The woman who answered the phone was the same one I'd talked to the day before.

I pitched my voice up half an octave and said, "I'm from the Oro *Gazette*. I didn't want to bother Mr. Adams about it, but I need his mother's birth date for the obituary column. Can you help me out?"

"Why, yes, I can," she said. "It was the second of March and she was, let's see, sixty-two, so the year was—"

"March," I said. "Are you sure?"

"Yes, but if you'd like to speak to Mr. Adams—"

"That won't be necessary," I said, and hung up.

Not only were Janet and Emmy close friends, they'd known each other long before Janet came to Oro. It seemed peculiar that nobody had mentioned that fact. Particularly that Greg hadn't mentioned it. Of course, he had just been hit with the news of his mother's death and I hadn't questioned him specifically about it. I decided to rectify that oversight right away. I could always use the necklace as an excuse to see him.

I looked up his address in the phone book, jotted it down on my note pad and started to get dressed, wishing I'd brought another change of clothes. For some irrational reason, I hated to go see Greg wearing the outfit I'd worn this morning at Bak's.

Stupid thing to worry about. He certainly wasn't going to pay any attention to the way I looked.

Still, I found myself digging around in the bottom of my purse for makeup and applying eye shadow with an out-of-practice hand. I was curling on mascara when the telephone let out a shrill ring. The wand jumped and deposited a black glob on my eyelid.

Damn. I blotted the excess on a washcloth as I went to answer the phone.

I hadn't told anybody where I was staying, but the icy voice on the other end of the line didn't surprise me at all.

"Mrs. West? Correct me if I'm wrong, but I was under the impression you were working for me. I don't like to have to track down employees."

"Sorry, Mr. Valek. I planned to call you as soon as I tied up some loose ends here."

"I don't like the sound of that. You were to check on Janet so you could reassure David. Nothing more. I want to see you immediately. Leave Oro right now and come here to my house in Newport Beach."

He hung up before I could explain anything about Janet and the situation I'd discovered.

Well, that's that, I thought.

I'd wanted off the case and I was about to get my

wish. I went into the bathroom and washed off the eye makeup, wondering why I was so disappointed. I didn't know if it was because I was beginning to get involved in the mystery surrounding Janet's disappearance or simply because I wouldn't be seeing Greg Adams again.

It's just as well, I thought, picking up the necklace and putting it in my purse.

I'll mail it to him, I decided as I packed my overnight bag and went to check out.

IT WAS A LONG HOT DRIVE from Oro, but by the time I got to Newport Beach, ocean breezes had moderated the temperature and added some humidity.

I had Valek's address from the personal check he had given me. My Orange County Thomas Guide pinpointed the location in the choicest part of town high on a hill with an ocean view overlooking Balboa Harbor. After a long drive through streets where large houses hid behind well-kept masses of tropical shrubbery, I found a gate with Valek spelled out in the ironwork.

It was open so I turned in, parked on the curved driveway and watched a DC-9 thunder by. In Newport for a million-five you get all the luxury of high-class suburbia and a running battle with the County over the jet noise from John Wayne Airport.

There were two other cars on the driveway. One was long and black, built along the lines of a hearse. Nice thought, but I had to give it up when the maid who answered the door said, "Senor Valek ees busy. Come later, *por favor*."

"I'll wait," I said, pushing past her.

She didn't put up much resistance. I guess after working for Valek she got used to being pushed around. She wrung her hands and darted frightened looks toward a set of closed double doors on the left side of the large rectangular hallway.

"Don't worry," I said, gesturing to a straight chair that stood next to an antique chest. "I'll just sit right here until Mr. Valek is free. *Gracias*."

After she scuttled away, I sat for a few minutes and stared at the wallpaper. On the other side of the double doors voices rumbled like the pounding of faraway surf. I was tired and hungry and since I was going to be fired anyway, I didn't see any sense sitting around and waiting politely.

I marched over and knocked on the door. The voices stopped and a moment later Valek swung it open, snarling, "Dammit, Maria, I told you—"

"Hope I'm not interrupting anything," I said. "But you sounded in a hurry to see me."

He gave me a look that would freeze over a hot tub. "I didn't give you permission to come barging in like this. I'll talk to you when I'm finished here. Wait outside."

The door was already swinging shut when the other man in the room came over, saying, "Just a minute, Larry. Is this the young woman who's checking on Janet?"

"Yes, I am," I said, stepping around Valek. "I'm Delilah West."

He hesitated before admitting, "Daniel Hodge."

He was a ruined hulk of a man. His chest had caved in, dragging his shoulders down with it. A once handsome face collapsed and hung in folds from cheek and jawbones, the skin ashy gray. Jailhouse pallor, I thought, but I'm not dumb enough to think he'd been locked away in solitary. More likely he'd spent his time in a white-collar prison doing nothing more strenuous than keeping his room clean. But if you looked in his eyes, you knew that what had happened to Daniel Hodge went beyond physical confinement.

"I'll handle this, Dan," Valek said brusquely. "After Mrs. West and I are through, I'll give you a call."

"I want to stay. I mean," Hodge said, the firmness in his voice melting like butter, "I'm as worried about Janet as you are, Larry, so—"

"I'm not worried at all," Valek declared.

"You ought to be," I said. "Janet's not in Oro. She disappeared three weeks ago."

"She did what? What do you mean, disappeared?"

"One day she was there and the next she was gone." I looked longingly at an arrangement of sofas in front of the fireplace. "Can we discuss this sitting down?"

Valek strode over to his desk and gestured toward a couple of hard-cushioned side chairs. "Damn that girl," he said, glaring at me across a yard of oiled teak. "I know she's determined to make my life hell, but to go running off again without one thought about David—where is she?"

"I don't know," I said.

"What have you been doing? I paid you to look for my daughter. I even told you where to find her. She's with that artist, Bak."

"Your information was wrong. Bak's in Oro, but Janet's not there. Anyway, she only lived with him for two weeks. Then she moved into town and got a job."

That stopped him for a moment. "I don't believe it. She's never worked a day in her life."

"She has now."

"Well, then," Hodge put in, "maybe she got a better job offer someplace else."

His chair was situated slightly behind me. I had to turn around to say, "Since people are not exactly beating the bushes for unskilled receptionists, I don't think there's much chance of that." I turned back to Valek. "Frankly, the thing that worries me is that this is not a part of her pattern. She's run away before, but she always came back here. This time she didn't. And there's something else. Yesterday the woman who rented a house to Janet was killed."

"You're not suggesting that this has anything to do with my daughter?"

"I think it might. Janet knew the woman before she went to Oro. Maybe you can tell me how well. The woman's name was Emmy Adams."

Valek froze. Hodge made a croaking sound but when I turned for a look he was blowing his nose on a tablecloth-size handkerchief and mumbling, "Sorry."

"You'd better go home, Dan," Valek said. "You know what the doctor said about getting overtired."

"I'm all right, Larry. I'll stay and hear what Mrs. West has to say about Janet."

The tension between the two men gave me the feeling that Hodge had run the original show. He wasn't quite used to playing second banana.

"No," Valek said firmly. "That's not a good idea. Anyway, Mrs. West is about finished." He gave me the full benefit of his icy stare. "Look, you're getting pretty far afield from what I hired you to do. For your information, I didn't know this Adams

woman and I doubt that Janet did. As for your in-
sinuation that her death is connected with my
daughter, I'm sure the police don't share your
opinion. Otherwise, they'd have been here to question me.''

He got up and walked around the desk. ''Come
on, Dan. I'll walk you to your car. I'll be back in a
few minutes, Mrs. West, to settle up your bill.''

For the second time that day I knew I was getting
the runaround. There was one person in the Valek
household who would give me a straight answer. I
went out in the hall and followed the sound of a
vacuum cleaner to Maria. She pointed me in the
direction of the pool.

David was swimming laps, cutting the water in
smooth efficient lines. As he turned at the end of
the pool, he saw me, treaded water while he flipped
his head to shake the wet hair out of his eyes and
then hoisted himself up on the deck.

''Mrs. West, I'm so glad to see you. I called your
office, but Mrs. Braddock said she hadn't heard
from you.'' He toweled his dripping body and
watched me anxiously. ''Did you see Janet? Is
she—''

''Let's sit down,'' I said, indicating an umbrellaed
table and chair set. ''David, when I got to Oro,
Janet had already left.''

''She had? Well, that's great. I mean, she must be
on her way home. Knowing Janet, she stopped off
someplace for a shopping spree. She'll buy me my
whole winter wardrobe and everything she can
think of that I like to eat and probably throw in a
marching band. Did you tell dad?''

I might have to deflate his bubble of happiness,
but I didn't have to like doing it. So I put it off and

nodded. "He was having a conference with Mr. Hodge. I'm afraid I barged in."

"That's funny," David said. "I didn't know Uncle Dan was here. He usually says hello. Oh, well, I'm sure he was glad to hear about Janet. He was worried about her."

"Are he and Janet close?"

"No. Not at all. I don't think Janet likes him very much. I don't, either, not really, but I feel sorry for him. He doesn't have any kids."

"David, I imagine you know most of Janet's friends. Did you know a Mrs. Adams? Emmy Adams? An older woman in her sixties. She was blind."

"Adams? No, I don't think Janet ever mentioned her. Why do you ask?"

"Because Mrs. West is taking her investigation just a bit too seriously," Valek said, moving up behind David. I'd been so intent on our conversation that I hadn't heard his approach. "I thought I told you to wait in the study," he said to me.

"So you did, but my job was to give David a report about his sister."

"And did you? Did you tell him she's run off again?"

I had to face David's stricken look. "What's he talking about, Mrs. West? Where's Janet?"

I reached over and took his hand. "David, she was over in Oro since June, but she left three weeks ago and nobody seems to know where she went."

"She must have been coming home. She knew I'd be back from Europe. She had an accident or got sick or something. Dad—"

"Now, son, you're jumping to conclusions." Valek put both hands on the boy's shoulders in a

comforting gesture. "She's just off on another fling.
I'll put somebody on it right away and find her."

"That'll take too much time," David said. "Mrs.
West is already working on the case."

"Not anymore," Valek said grimly. "I think she
has too many prior commitments."

"Is that true?" David asked. "Please, Mrs. West.
I'd really like you to help find Janet."

"You've got my word on it. And about those prior
commitments," I said to Valek with my biggest,
sweetest smile. "I think I just might be able to wrig-
gle out of them."

9

AFTER I LEFT THE VALEKS, I stopped and called Rita. She said she could take a break and agreed to meet me at Mama Gonzales in an hour. That gave me enough time to stop by my apartment, pack a suitcase and change my clothes. After a moment's hesitation, I took my gun along, locking it in the glove compartment. I was on time, but Rita was already parked out in front of the small café.

Located on the edge of the Santa Ana barrio, Mama Gonzales could have been a shoe-repair store, a tailor shop or a dry cleaners. In fact, at one time or another it had been all three. Now it was full of cheap Formica tables and slippery vinyl chairs. A kitchen was in plain view behind a counter. If you had to have a menu, a misspelled, dimly typed, grease-stained copy could be found after an intensive search. Anything you ordered from it would be the best Mexican food in town.

Rita was drinking Tecate beer and drumming her fingers on the green-checked oilcloth that covered the tables. "You sure took your time," she said sharply. "What's going on?"

"In a minute," I said, signaling the waiter.

Gonzales had been a mom-and-pop operation with mama cooking and papa serving the food until he died. Now the children took turns filling in for him.

Today it was Ernesto in skin-tight jeans and a
T-shirt that read, Chicanos Make Better Lovers.

"Hey, Delilah," he said. "Where you been? You
on a diet or something?"

"Not by choice," I assured him. "How quick can
you get me a quesadilla and a beer?"

"*Inmediatamente*," he promised.

He was as good as his word and got mama working
on some chili rellenos while I attacked the Mexican
pizza of flour tortilla and melted cheese.

"Anytime you feel you can take a break from
stuffing your face," Rita said, "I'd like to know
why you've been incommunicado."

"Sorry." I wiped drips with a paper napkin and
told her that I'd found out Janet was not in Oro. I
finished up with a brief summary of Emmy Adams's
death, leaving out my suspicions that it was
murder.

"I don't like the sound of this," she said. "You
say you just happened to be there and dragged this
Mrs. Adams out of the house. But I read you pretty
well, Delilah, and I know that's not all of it."

I sighed. "There's so little I can nail down, Rita.
Mostly it's just a feeling something's wrong."

"So tell me and I'll judge for myself."

She listened silently, her square face growing
more and more grim. When I told her about Janet
and Emmy's friendship and asked if she recognized
the older woman's name, she shook her head.

"Listen, kiddo," she said urgently. "I want you to
level with me. What do you think happened to
Janet?"

I avoided her eyes. "I don't know."

"You don't know or you don't want to say? Do
you think she's dead?"

There was a wedge of quesadilla left on the plate. Grease filmed the cold cheese. Carefully I pushed it away. "I'm afraid she might be," I admitted.

"Dammit!" Her eyes were bright with tears. She blew her nose and swallowed a few times before she asked, "This Mrs. Adams—she knew something, so she was killed, too?"

"That's the way it adds up to me, Rita. I could be wrong. Everybody keeps telling me I am."

Ernesto put a plate in front of me with a flourish. The spicy aroma of chilis and refried beans started a wave of nausea. "Tell your mama I'm sorry," I said. "It looks delicious, but I don't think I can manage it right now."

I stood up and grabbed my purse. Put some money on the table. Headed for the door. Rita followed as I quickly covered the distance to my car.

"Are you all right?" she asked.

I nodded and got in the Pinto, rolled down the window. There was nothing I wanted more than to go back to my apartment, pull down the shades and drink enough margaritas to block Janet Valek and the whole damned mess out of my mind.

But when Rita bent down and said, "What are you going to do, Delilah? Are you giving up on this?" I shook my head.

"Not this time," I said above the roar of the engine. "I'm on my way back to Oro."

THE LATE AFTERNOON TRAFFIC filled the freeways like some gigantic hemorrhage, coagulating rapidly to block all the main arterial highways. I inched along, listening to my car gobbling gasoline, until I got to Route 71. Once I made the exit and headed south, the traffic eased up. Still, it was five o'clock when I arrived at the Old Prospector's Motel.

"I wish I'd known you were coming back," the manager said as he handed me a key. "There was a fellow looking for you. Tall, dark hair. He didn't leave his name."

Philip Hunter, I guessed. I called El Rancho Realty from my room and found I was right.

"The manager said you'd checked out," he said. "You promised to call and keep me informed."

"I know I did. Sorry. A few things came up."

"No, I'm the one who should apologize. I heard about Emmy. God, if only we'd gone over there when we first got to Janet's place. Or if I'd gone over with you instead of rushing off. It's useless to brood about it, I guess. It won't bring Emmy back. I always thought Greg was crazy to let her live alone. He was just asking for an accident like that."

"It wasn't an accident," I said.

"Wasn't—what are you talking about? You don't think this had anything to do with Janet?"

"Yes, I do. I found out that Janet knew Emmy before she came to Oro. I suspect they were old friends."

"But she never said a word to me about it. Did you tell the sheriff about this?"

"About my suspicions concerning Emmy's death. I found out the rest later. I was hoping to go out there right now and catch him before he left for the day."

"I don't think you'll have much luck. I drove by the station a little while ago. They've got some kind of open house going on. Just about everybody in town is there. I think I even saw Felix's truck parked out in front. God, he's got his nerve," he said bitterly.

"I talked to Felix this morning," I said.

"Did you get anything out of him?"

"Not much."

It occurred to me that Philip was asking most of the questions. His concern for Janet didn't automatically delete his name from my suspect list. He had admitted his jealousy. Maybe Janet decided to dump him for somebody else and he went a little crazy. It happens. It happens a lot.

"Listen, Philip, I've still got some checking to do. We'll talk again later."

He gave me an argument, but I finally got rid of him. Then I sat and stared at the phone for a while, trying to decide what to do. Finally I dragged out the phone book. There was no answer at Greg's office and his house was unlisted.

Maybe he's at a funeral parlor, I thought bleakly. Would there be a wake? An open coffin revealing his mother's cold waxy face?

I shuddered and ran out of the room, digging car keys from my purse. I stopped with my hand on the door handle. Where did I think I was going? It was senseless to go rushing off like this. I had to think the thing through, make some plans. I put away the keys and went to see if the motel café's coffee was as bad as I remembered it.

It was, but apple pie cut the taste a little. My booth faced the door. I saw Greg Adams as soon as he walked in. He wore faded Levi's, a plaid shirt open at the throat, scuffed boots. I had been right. His trim body looked much more comfortable than it had in a suit.

The waitress came over, menu in hand, as he sat

down opposite me, his eyes as coldly gray as a winter sea. "Nothing," he said, and waited until she was gone before he spoke again. "John Bell called me. You just couldn't leave it alone, could you?"

"What did he say?"

"That you came to him with your crazy idea. But it seems you added something new to your suspicions since you talked to me. Now you think Emmy's death is connected in some way to Janet's so-called disappearance. I don't know what you're trying to prove here, Mrs. West, but I'm damn well fed up with it."

I toyed with my coffee cup and wished his words didn't sting quite so much. "Look," I said. "It's a bad time for you right now. I understand and there's nothing I'd like better than to drop the whole thing. But I can't do that. There are too many unanswered questions."

"Such as?"

"Why didn't you tell me that Janet and your mother were old friends?"

A muscle twitched in his jaw. "I don't know what you're talking about," he said, turning away to wave the waitress over. She was busy with another customer and didn't see his signal.

"I have something to give to you," I said, opening my purse. I took out Emmy's necklace.

"Where did you get this?"

"I didn't steal it. Your mother was wearing it yesterday. The chain broke when I . . . when I pulled her from the kitchen. I found it on the floor. I was planning to mail it to you."

His hand closed around the gold chain. His face was unreadable so I went on. "The design on the pendant is Pisces. I believe your mother was born on March second.''

"You ought to know. You called my office this morning and pretended to be from the *Gazette*, didn't you?''

"Subterfuge seems to be the only way I can get any information.''

"So now you know Emmy's birthday. What on earth has that got to do with anything?''

"The necklace wasn't the only interesting thing I found in your mother's house. Janet sent her a birthday card. A special one in Braille.''

"There's only one way you could know that.'' His voice was taut with fury. "Who gave you permission to paw through my mother's things?''

"Getting angry is not going to sidetrack me,'' I said quietly. "I freely admit I'm a snoop, Mr. Adams. That's how I make my living. The point here is not how I found the card but what it means.''

"All right.'' He dropped the necklace into his shirt pocket and massaged his temples with long, square-tipped fingers. "Look, I suppose you mean well. But you're like a runaway horse. You've got the bit in your teeth and you're off in a wild gallop. Eventually you'll run out of steam, but while you're at it a lot of people get trampled in the stampede. Not only me. How about Janet's family? This must be terribly upsetting for them.''

"They were worried before they hired me.''

"I'm sure they were, but it's got to be worse if you're telling them your theories about Emmy's death. For God's sake, you make it sound like murder. And for what? Janet sent her a birthday card. Okay, maybe she did. Maybe your deduction's right. They were old friends. How do you get from there to the idea of somebody killing Emmy?''

"Janet's gone," I said. "Philip thinks she's dead. Everybody says he's crazy but let's suppose he's right. Unless she's a victim of a random killing, there has to be a motive. What if Janet became a threat to somebody because of something she heard or saw? And what if she confided in your mother?''

"There's only one thing wrong with your theory. Janet is not dead," he said emphatically.

"You're very sure of that. I'd like to know why.''

"It's obvious. Nobody's discovered her body.''

"There's a lot of wild country out here," I said. "A shallow grave on a deserted hillside—''

"No," he said. "It's not true and I'm not going to sit here and listen to any more of this." He stood up, hesitated and stared down at me. "Sometime I'd like to know what makes you have such dark and bloody visions, Delilah West. Whatever it is, you're letting it warp your judgment. There's no case here. The sooner you realize that the better it will be for all of us.''

I SAT IN MY MOTEL ROOM with its twenty-watt lighting and tried to drown out the memory of Greg's words with the inane chatter of a TV talk show.

Was he right? Was I letting my past encounters with violence pervert my judgment? Maybe I identified with Janet too much. It was easy to imagine that some past trauma haunted her eyes or that she had become the tragic victim of murder. But what did I really know about the woman?

Every person I'd talked to saw her differently. She was headstrong and thoughtless. Considerate and loving. Promiscuous. Another woman. A loyal friend.

A burst of applause greeted a guest who swivel-hipped her way across the TV screen to join Merv. From the minute she opened her mouth you knew her cleavage was the only thing she had going for her. I shut off the set and paced the silent room.

An awful lot of people thought I was nuts. Maybe they were right, but the doubt stuck like a burr in the folds of my brain. At this point it would take a frontal lobotomy to get it out. Tomorrow I'd start all over again and question everybody. I'd start with Felix Bak. He'd remembered something. I was sure of it. Something to do with the night that Janet disappeared.

I looked at my watch. Ten o'clock. I was too full of coffee and adrenalin to sleep. Instinct told me that Felix was a night person, so why wait until tomorrow to question him?

I left the motel and headed for Mesquite Canyon, stopping at a Night Owl Market to buy some alcoholic lubricant for Bak's rusty memory. Once I left the artificial glow of Oro, night closed in with stars crisp and hard overhead against an inky blackness. I drove slowly looking for potholes. I even managed to avoid one or two.

At least I didn't miss the turnoff. Finding the entrance to the canyon was another matter. I crept along looking for Bak's artist palette signpost and wishing I'd had enough sense to wait until morning. I was past the canyon road before I saw the sign, so I had to brake and back up. As I swung around the corner, my headlights struck a glint off something metallic, but I was too busy concentrating on my driving to give it more than a passing thought.

I jolted over the last stretch of washboard and pulled up beside the Ranchero. A dim light burned in the back studio, but the front of the house was dark. At least he's home, I thought, reaching for the door handle. Then I remembered the dog and hesitated. Did his protective instincts get any sharper after sundown? I tooted the horn for Felix. There was no response from him and still no sign of the dog.

Warily I stepped out of the car, listening for sounds of the animal's approach. There was nothing. Only a silence so complete it hurt my straining ears. I shivered in desert-cooled night air and wondered briefly why I wasn't tucked in bed in some nice surburban house with a nine-to-five husband and a couple of kids asleep down the hall.

There was no sign of the mutt. Some watchdog, I thought, walking between my Pinto and the Ranchero.

Just in front of the pickup, my foot struck something large and unyielding. I staggered, lost my balance and fell. At the same moment, orange light winked from the porch. Then a bullet split the air above me and slammed into the Ranchero's windshield.

10

I CROUCHED IN THE DARKNESS with the sound of the whining bullet echoing in my head and my heart pounding raggedly.

Felix, I thought. The damn fool is probably high. If I hadn't stumbled. . . .

My hand touched the obstacle that had saved my life. Rough fur. Smooth muzzle, velvety smooth by contrast to the coarse unkempt coat. Something sticky and warm along the ridge of nose. I jerked my hand away, but it was too late. My fingers had brushed the spot above the eyes where the hard skull felt soft and mushy.

No wonder the dog hadn't barked when I drove up. I felt along the body for a heartbeat, but I knew I wouldn't find it.

The man's gone crazy, I thought, trying to pierce the black shadows of the porch. The dog barked once too often and Felix clubbed him to death. I could almost hear him roaring in rage and see him swinging a rock or a gun butt at the poor animal.

I'd picked a wonderful time to drop in. God knows what he was tripping on. Acid. P.C.P. My mouth and throat ached with dryness. I swallowed painfully and tried to decide what would be the least suicidal way to get out of this mess.

Maybe I should talk to him, I thought and discarded the idea immediately.

During my stint with the L.A.P.D. I'd seen a few freaked-out characters, enough to convince me that I didn't want to tangle with one who had a gun in his hand. All right then, if I couldn't talk, I had to run.

I looked over at my car. It was about twenty feet away but it seemed like a hundred. Instead of pulling directly next to the Ranchero, I'd parked at about a forty-five degree angle and there was only one tiny bump of rock in between to provide any kind of cover.

What about the Ranchero? If the keys were in the ignition, it would be my best bet. But if they weren't? At this point, Felix hadn't seen me moving since the first shot. Maybe he thought I was dead. Whichever vehicle I chose for escape, there would be a moment of exposure when I opened the door and the interior light went on. Better to take a chance on a sure thing. Anyway there was a gun in my car, locked in the glove compartment. I'd feel a hell of a lot better with that gun in my hand.

If I crawled back to the pickup's back bumper and approached my car from the rear, the bulk of the truck would provide a shield for most of the maneuver. I didn't let myself consider opening the door. I only thought about afterward. Once inside, I'd keep my head below the windshield, take a chance on swinging blindly around in back of the Ranchero, hoping the pickup would stop most of the bullets.

Okay. The car was it. Now all I needed was the keys to the ignition.

I remembered dropping them into my purse just

before I tripped. As I fell, the purse flew out of my hands. Pray they stayed inside it. My pupils had dilated now, adjusting to the darkness, so I picked out the purse easily, a bulky shadow next to the truck's front wheel. I inched around the mutt, steeling myself against the doggy smell of his fur, the odor of feces voided in the moment of death.

The flesh on my palms stung as I pulled myself along the rough sand. Scrapes. Skin burns. Forget it. Think what a bullet hole would have done.

I picked up the purse and crawled toward the back of the truck. It's a huge purse. Usually well organized. Not tonight. While I searched its various compartments, I realized there was still no sound from the dark cave of the porch. Maybe Felix had gone inside.

No. Impossible. The front door had a rusty creak that would shatter this stillness. He was there in the shadows, waiting quietly. Too quietly.

The skin between my shoulder blades tightened. When was a freaked-out acidhead ever so quiet? High-pitched giggles, babbling incoherence, frenetic activity were much more typical. The tightening grew to icy stabs of fear.

"Felix?" I screamed. "Felix?"

A faint scratch of shoes, a whisper of clothing as he shifted position. Then silence so complete it was like somebody had clamped down a big dome to enclose the space between me and the house. The only sound was the thud of my heartbeat that vibrated my eardrums and hurt the back of my throat.

Find the keys, I directed my clumsy fingers, damning the infinite number of corners in the large pouch. If they'd fallen out on the sandy earth—my fingers touched the familiar metal shape and I could have cried in relief.

I clenched a fist around them, knotted my other hand in the purse strap and began the slow crawl toward my car. Careful. Only one chance to do it right. Think about the sequence. Open the door. Inside as quickly as possible. Key in the ignition. *Now.*

I reached for the door handle, bracing myself for the wash of light, but it was—oh, God—like a spotlight, blinding me with brilliance. The gun on the porch flashed. Once. Twice. The side window exploded, showering me with glass shards. Another bullet tore into metal inches away, pulling the door from my hand and slamming it shut.

I dived for the scant shelter of the small pinnacle of rock, hugging the ground, hands over my head in a futile gesture of protection.

Gunfire echoed and re-echoed off the canyon walls. Angry spits of bullets kicked up a shower of sand. One ricocheted from the rock with a ping, chipping stone splinters.

My insides turned to jelly. Visions of torn flesh, of shredded arteries pumping blood, of spilled entrails paralyzed my judgment for a long moment before I realized the gunfire had stopped.

Don't move, the fear told me. He's waiting, just waiting. No, he's reloading. It's now or never.

The car keys were gone, lost somewhere in the darkness. There was another set taped to the firewall beneath the hood. No way to get to those. No chance to drive away or to reach my gun. I wondered why I'd ever thought the night was so dark. Starlight glittered on the ground like discarded tinsel. Might as well have been high noon it was so bright.

I plunged blindly across the narrow, sandy strip toward the truck, gunfire nipping my heels before I rammed head-on into the side of the pickup. The gun flashed again. I felt a burning slash along the upper part of my arm as though I'd touched a live wire.

I screamed, fell flat on my face and rolled under the truck. Pain exploded so viciously I felt myself teeter on the edge of consciousness. I willed away the blackness, spit out sand, turned on my back to relieve the pressure. Grabbed my arm above the elbow and squeezed hard to try and block out the feeling.

A flesh wound. Shoot 'em ups and showdowns at the O.K. Corral. A flesh wound in the best western tradition. That's all it was.

But my hand was sticky with blood and I had no way of knowing for sure. I took a deep breath, tried to sublimate the pain and concentrate on my situation. The last spate of gunfire had come from the right side of the house.

He's moving, I thought. Circling.

He. Definitely not Felix Bak. An anonymous killer trapped in the box canyon and desperate.

He must know by now that I didn't have a gun. From my scream he'd assume I was hit. If I lay very still, if I made no move at all, maybe he'd think I was dead. He'd keep circling, moving, trying to escape.

To hell with the risk of opening the truck door, looking for keys. I pressed my ear against the sandy earth and waited, listening for any sound that would tell me he was leaving.

As if the whole world was holding its breath and then letting it out with a sigh, a rustle shook the mesquite trees. My skin crawled as the sound increased, rattling the seed pods together with faint clicks. Night wind. Swirling drafts of cooler air invading the narrow confines of the canyon.

Son of a bitch. I couldn't hear a thing that might indicate his passing. The damn wind obliterated any sound of shoes against sand and stone.

I lay there, feeling blood soak into my blouse. An eternity passed. Two eternities. Then there was a distant growl of an engine turning over. The roar of a gunned accelerator, the diminishing sound of a car driving away into the night.

He was gone. It had to be him. The reflection I saw when I turned into the canyon was a glint of chrome from a car hidden there. I knew logically it was so, but I didn't believe it. My skin vibrated with the feeling that he was still lurking in the shadows. I lay, shivering, smelling the oily underside of the truck, afraid to move.

Slowly the trembling stopped. My arm hurt like hell. I could feel blood dripping off my fingers where I gripped it. I thought I should get to the house and stem the flow before I bled to death, so I slid out from under the truck carefully, using my good elbow to pull me along.

The night breeze touched me and I shivered again, but this time from cold. Cautiously I worked my way around the truck.

If he's still out there, I thought, knowing he wasn't. But if....

I pushed away from the truck and ran toward the house, zigzagging to avoid fire that never came. I grabbed a post on the porch to hold myself upright and gasped for air.

Stupid. Damn fool. He left minutes ago. Hours.

I staggered up the steps, pushed open the door. I didn't think about Felix. I hadn't wanted to think about him because I knew what I would find.

Felix. Arms thrown out in a futile gesture, he lay in the doorway to the studio. Paint-bright blood made an abstract design around him that rivaled the canvases on the wall.

11

THERE WAS NOTHING I COULD DO for Felix. I couldn't tell where he had been shot without moving the body, but all that bright arterial blood indicated the bullet had struck something vital.

I turned on some lights in the outer room and assessed my own wound. It didn't look as bad as it felt, just an angry furrow plowed through the flesh about two inches down from the shoulder. I went over to the tiny kitchen and washed off the dirt and dried blood. That started the bleeding up again. There was nothing in the house clean enough to use for a bandage. I grabbed some paper towels and pressed them against it, setting my teeth against the pain.

Antibiotics, I thought and tetanus—when was the last time I had a tetanus shot? Some painkillers wouldn't hurt, either.

I didn't feel like driving, but there was no telephone in the place. I had to get back to town, find a doctor, call the police.

My eyes went unwillingly to Felix's body. I was beginning to go hot and cold and there was a buzzing in my ears. I looked around and spotted a bottle of Scotch that shared the kitchen counter with about a year's worth of dirty dishes. A long swallow left me gasping, but at least I didn't pass out.

After a few more precautionary sips, I let my mind slip up slowly on the subject of the killer. Who was he? Why had he killed Felix? There was nothing to help identify him. He was as unseen and deadly as the gas that crept through Mrs. Adams's house.

I looked around the room. Disorder was its natural state so it was hard to tell, but it looked as though it had been searched. The neatly kept studio confirmed it. Carefully I stepped around the body and went in for a look. Doors were open. Drawers pulled out and dumped. It certainly looked like a robbery.

Philip had told me it had happened before. Hopped-up kids looking for an easy score. But that kind of crime generates chaos. This felt slick, planned. Don't ask me why. A feeling again, and who was going to believe a feeling? I believed it and knew this wasn't robbery. It was murder. Felix did remember something. The killer made sure nobody would find out what it was.

I turned away, my glance touching the large cupboard, the one that held the nude paintings. It had been left untouched, padlock in place. Maybe I'd interrupted the killer before he had time to find the key or smash the lock.

I remembered the coarsely sensual painting of Janet that Felix had shown me. God knows what would happen to it once a police investigation started. Lawrence Valek would be furious if it went on public display. I didn't give a damn about Valek, but it did matter to me that David would be hurt.

If the key to the cupboard was on Felix's body, it would have to stay there. I couldn't bring myself to touch him. When a cursory search failed to uncover it, I looked around for something to pry off the lock. I found nothing stronger than a screwdriver so I used it to take the hasp off instead.

There were five paintings in the cupboard done on twenty-four by thirty-six stretched canvas, all unframed. I flipped through them, looking for the one of Janet, and stopped as I recognized the painted image of Claire Ingram.

I slid it from the cupboard, both fascinated and repelled by the devastating portrait. The pose was that of a shy young girl, but lines cracked a rapacious face; dried breasts hung from a bony chest; thin gray hair outlined the detailed pubic mound. It was a woman's oldest nightmare of the ravages of age. No wonder Claire got upset when I mentioned Bak's paintings.

I kept it out along with the one of Janet. Maybe it would buy me a little cooperation. Maybe I just felt sorry for the woman. Whatever the reason, I took both paintings with me to the kitchen.

The paper towel was bloody by then so I tore off some more, wadding it into a thick pad. I needed something to hold it in place while I drove, but I didn't want to touch anything in that filthy place. With some difficulty, I ripped off the hem of my blouse and used the strip of cloth to tie on the makeshift bandage.

I couldn't stall any longer. I had to go back out into the darkness. Over by the front door a huge chrome flashlight hung on a nail. I took it down, flicked on the switch, and juggled it and the paintings out the door.

With the help of the strong light, I easily located my purse. The car keys were another matter. I gave up looking when the light swept the mound of dark

fur and revealed the dog's crushed head. I opened
the Pinto's hood and peeled off the black friction
tape that held an extra set of keys in place. Then I
locked the paintings in the trunk and opened the
car door. Most of the window was gone. Only a few
jagged remnants remained. I knocked them out
with the edge of my purse. Then I used it like a
shovel to brush glass fragments from the seat, got in
gingerly and drove away.

The potholes in the dirt road seemed to have
multiplied. Every jounce made my arm throb. When
my wheels finally touched pavement, I swore I'd
never complain about highway taxes again.

At the intersection of Route 71, I stopped and
debated. I doubted whether the small town had a
hospital. I hadn't seen one. I could drive back to my
motel, call a doctor from there, but the sheriff's
substation was closer.

Two officers sat at the front desk, drinking coffee
and monitoring communications. They took one
look at me and sprang into action. One got out a
first-aid kit and used it on my arm with expert care.
As soon as I gave them an abbreviated report of
what had happened in Mesquite Canyon, the other
one got on the radio and ordered a patrol car to investigate. He must have called the sheriff, too,
because by the time the first one finished winding
gauze around the the cleaned wound, John Bell
walked in.

He wore khaki pants and a sweat shirt. Behind
the metal-rimmed glasses, his eyes were bruised
with tired shadows. Gray whiskers stubbled a long
jaw. He'd combed his hair but the part was crooked
and a stubborn tuft stuck up near the crown.

"You send a car out to Bak's place?" he asked the
officer behind the desk.

"On its way."

He turned to me. "Are you all right?"

"I've been better." I looked down at my blood-stained blouse. "I've looked better, too."

"Hank," Bell said to my first-aid attendant, "you got a shirt in your locker Ms. West could borrow?"

"Sure thing. I'll go get it."

"Thanks," I said.

"Why don't you change in my office?" Bell said. "I'll be with you in a minute."

The clean shirt felt wonderful next to my skin once I got my arm through the sleeve. I was just finishing with the buttons when Bell knocked politely and came in. He stopped at a file cabinet, took a bottle of Wild Turkey from one of the drawers, and brought it over to the desk along with two paper cups.

"You up to a few questions?" he asked, handing me a cup filled to the brim.

I nodded and sipped some of the whiskey.

"What were you doing out in Mesquite Canyon in the middle of the night?"

"I went to see Felix earlier today—yesterday—what time is it, anyway? My watch must have stopped."

"One forty-five. I assume this visit was to question him about Janet Valek?"

"It certainly wasn't a social call."

"What did he tell you about her?"

"Not a lot," I said. "He started moving in on me as soon as I walked in. Then suddenly he was in a big hurry to get rid of me. The more I thought about it the more I became convinced that he'd remembered something about the night she disappeared. I went out there to ask him."

"Bad business, walking into an armed robbery."

"If that's what it was."

"Nothing else it could be," he said firmly. "Everybody in town knows Bak was into drugs. Hell, he's been busted twice. Kids are always drifting up and down this route, especially with the Interstate going in. Vans, motorcycles—Christ," he said, shaking his head and taking a mouthful of whiskey as if to wash away a bad taste. "Easy enough to pick up information about Bak. It's not the first time he was robbed."

"Sounds like your mind's made up," I said. After he saw the ransacked interior of Bak's house, he'd be even more convinced, so I added, "Everybody knew about that earlier robbery, too. It makes a neat cover for murder."

"Why did I know you were going to say that?" The mild blue eyes iced over and the jaw hardened. "This investigation will follow all proper procedures," he said coldly. "That includes keeping an open mind about all possibilities. But I'm not going to be a party to some kind of witch hunt just on your woman's intuition."

His tone said it all. So much for his polite veneer of equality and his careful *Ms.* West.

"I'm a great believer in intuition," I said, matching his frigid tone. "So was my husband, only he called it playing a hunch. Whatever label you stick on it, yes, I do have a feeling it was murder. Probably done by the same person who killed Emmy Adams, and for almost the same reason."

"To keep him from telling what he remembered— what you have a *feeling* he remembered." He picked up a pen, drew over a note pad. "Everything in the Adams case points to an accident. Now, why don't you help me get to the real reason for Bak's death by giving me some solid information? See any other vehicles in the area?''

"None except Bak's Ranchero, but I heard the killer drive away, and I'm sure his car was parked outside the canyon. He came in on foot."

"We'll check it out," he said noncommittally. "All right, you drove to Bak's—then what happened?"

"I parked, got out, started for the house. It was very dark. I stumbled—" I broke off and took a big gulp of the whiskey. "The dog was lying there, dead. I tripped over him and it probably saved my life."

"You have a gun?"

"I own one. It was locked in the glove compartment so it didn't do me any good."

"You get any look at all at the sniper?"

"None. It was very dark out. There were no lights on in the front of the house, and he was on the porch where it was pitch black."

He led me quickly and expertly through the rest of it. I managed a fairly coherent story but the aftereffects of shock combined with the liquor I'd consumed was catching up fast. A kind of hazy numbness seemed to fill my head. Bell kept fading in and out. I had to blink hard to keep him in focus.

By the time I finished with a description of the condition of the house, it was like listening to your own voice on a cheap tape recorder. I heard myself say, "So I took the paintings and—" With an enormous effort I turned off the words, my insides quivering at how close I'd come to telling him about the paintings in the trunk of my car. "I mean, I took a look at the paintings and. . .I forgot what I was going to say. Don't you have enough for now? I'm really exhausted."

He nodded and stood up. "You'd better have a doctor check that arm," he said. "I'll get Hank to call Carl Jessup. Carl's used to emergencies."

"How do I find him?"

"Just off Main Street, two blocks this side of the Old Prospector's Motel," he said, and escorted me into the outer office.

Even though I was stumbling around in a daze, I got the message. He'd made it his business to find out where I was staying and now he wanted me to know it. The gloves were off for good.

Bell finished his instructions to Hank with, "Tell them I'm on my way." Then he turned to me. "I'll expect you back here first thing in the morning for an official statement."

"Fine," I said to his back as the front door closed behind him. All I wanted to do was lie down on the hard tiled floor and go to sleep.

"You okay?" Hank asked. "The doctor's expecting you. Maybe I ought to run you over there."

"No, thanks. I can manage." To prove it I walked to the door without falling down. It seemed to take a long time and something nagged at my memory with every step. "Officer, there was a dog killed out at Bak's place. . . ."

He nodded. "I heard about that from the patrol. Don't worry. I'll have one of the men bury him."

BY THE TIME I DROVE BACK to the motel, it was three-thirty. A sliver of moon rode the eastern horizon. Smoke from a fire burning in the San Jacinto Mountains made it look like a slice of pale cantaloupe. Chill desert air poured in through the missing window, an acrid smell of ash overlaying the fragrance of hopsage. I hunched my shoulders against the cold, shivering, my teeth clacking together.

The doctor had mumbled sleepily that Hank Weems was as good as they come at dressing a wound. He left the bandage alone and told me to come back tomorrow and have it changed. Then he gave me a tetanus shot and a bottle of Darvon and told me to get some rest.

So now both arms hurt like hell as I parked the car and let myself into the cold motel room. I turned on a wall heater to the highest setting and staggered over to the bed. I wanted to take a pain pill but after all the liquor I decided it wasn't the smartest thing to do. I was too tired to get undressed so I kicked off my shoes and wrapped up in a blanket.

Eventually I stopped shaking and the pain dimmed like turning down a light with a rheostat. But before that happened I had a lot of time to think.

They were nasty thoughts. Graphic and bloody.

Two people were dead. Regardless of what Bell believed, I didn't buy accident or robbery. Somebody had turned on the gas in Mrs. Adams's kitchen and deliberately sneaked in to shoot Felix. Their involvement with Janet was the thing that linked the killings.

Coincidence? I had a feeling that John Bell was going to call it that and sweep it under the rug. And me along with it if I didn't watch out.

12

I DREAMED OF A FACELESS KILLER stalking me across burning deserts, and awoke to find the temperature in the room hovering around ninety-five. After shutting off the wall heater and turning on the air conditioner, I stumbled into the bathroom and tried to quench a raging thirst with tepid tap water.

. The bandage on my arm was still in good shape. Apparently the wound had stayed closed. There was only a dull throb until I tried to bathe and wash my hair.

A sticker on the bathroom mirror declared that a water-saving device had been installed in the shower head to Conserve California's Most Precious Resource. The resulting trickle was pretty good for keeping bandages dry but was hell on one-handed shampooing.

By the time I towel dried my hair and struggled into a dress, my arm pounded furiously. I took a couple of Darvon and went to the café to see if some of their horrible coffee would jolt my brain cells into action.

There was nothing in the morning paper about Bak's death, but the memory was grimly clear as I left the café, walked over to my car and looked at the missing window, a bullet hole in the door, fragments of glass on the seat and floors.

My watch still wasn't working—another casualty, I thought—but I knew it was past nine o'clock. I headed out of town toward the substation, intending to get the statement out of the way. I put my foot on the brake as I neared the building, hesitated, then accelerated straight ahead. I couldn't afford to pass up the chance to spring the news of Bak's murder on Claire and Philip and watch their reaction. Sheriff Bell would have to wait.

Philip's green Seville was the lone car parked in front of the office. Good, I thought. Easier to judge reactions one at a time.

He was in the reception area digging through a file cabinet as I came in the door.

"Delilah," he said, abandoning his search, his dark eyes full of concern. "Are you all right? I heard about Felix. God, what a thing for you to walk into. Here, sit down."

So much for catching him off guard. I waited for him to stop fussing over the seating arrangement to ask, "How did you hear about it?"

He settled his lanky body behind the desk and said, "One of the patrolmen was in the coffee shop this morning. He'd just come from Mesquite Canyon. He said somebody was hitting Felix for dope again and things got out of hand."

"That seems to be the official version."

"You don't believe it?"

"I was there. The killer didn't act like a drug-crazed kid to me."

"Well, it really doesn't matter who it was," he said. "He deserves a medal as far as I'm concerned, except for one thing. How the hell are we going to find out what happened to Janet now that Felix is dead?"

"Did you ever consider the possibility that you were wrong about him?"

"Somebody got to you," he said. A strand of black hair fell across his forehead. He fingercombed it impatiently back in place. "You think I'm crazy, just like everybody else."

"That's not what I said. You may be right about Janet. I'm beginning to think you are. But what if somebody else was responsible for her disappearance? The same person who killed Emmy Adams and Felix."

"My God," he said, stunned. "I don't believe it. I mean, I wouldn't put anything past Felix, but who would do something like that? And for what possible reason?"

"They knew something about Janet's disappearance and somebody wanted to shut them up."

"I don't know," he said, but he was shaking his head and it was clear that his mind was made up. "I appreciate the fact that you're the only one who would listen to me, but I think you're way off base with this. I hear that Felix's place was ripped apart, and it was obviously a robbery."

"How about Claire? Does she make it unanimous?"

"We didn't discuss it. She remembered some errands and went out right away."

I'll bet, I thought, sure that one of the errands involved the painting locked in the trunk of my car.

"I'd better be going too," I said, searching for an excuse. "The sheriff wanted a statement first thing this morning."

"Well, then, maybe I'd better say goodbye just in case I don't see you again."

"Why do you think you won't see me?"

"I assumed since the case has come to a dead end, you'd be leaving Oro."

"It's not over yet," I said. "There's still one or two things I want to check out. How about you, Philip? What are you going to say to Bell when he questions you about Felix's murder?"

"Why should he do that?"

"He's hung up on this robbery angle, but he strikes me as a pretty thorough man. You haven't exactly kept your feelings about Felix a secret. Do you have an alibi for last night?"

"Well, no," he said, looking flustered. "I was feeling pretty crummy so I stayed home all evening. But it's ridiculous to think I'd have anything to do with it. Sure, I'd like to have beaten the truth out of him about Janet, but to kill him. . . . You don't really consider me a suspect?"

"Everybody's a suspect," I said, and made a fast exit before he could protest anymore.

IT WAS A LONG WAY from the dark ride of the night before as I bumped over the road to Mesquite Canyon. The sun beat down, hot and bright, but there was a hollow spot in my chest that grew colder and colder as I followed the arrow on the sign and turned toward Bak's house.

The Ranchero sat in the same spot, its windshield starred with bullet holes. A blue Datsun 280Z was parked next to it. Claire, I thought, not a bit surprised. I pulled in on the other side of the truck, my eyes going automatically to the ground in front of it, afraid of what I would see. Thank God, the dog's body was gone. I hoped that Officer Weems had kept his promise.

The feeling of dread intensified as I approached

the house. My brain knew the sniper was gone, that
Felix's body was in cold storage in the morgue, but
somehow the message was not getting through to
my nerve endings.

A placard on the front door announced: Sheriff's
Investigation in Progress. NO ADMITTANCE. But
the knob turned beneath my hand and the door
swung open.

Sounds indicated a frantic search was going on
in the studio. Something heavy thumped against
the floor. A cupboard door slammed. The noise
covered my entry and progress across the outer
room.

Chalk outlined the spot in the studio doorway
where the corpse had lain, but it wasn't necessary.
The blood had been absorbed by the soft wood and
a dark, purplish stain marked the floor. Firmly
checking my squirming insides, I edged around the
outline and entered the studio.

Sunlight streamed in through the window intensi-
fying the garish explosion of color on the walls.
Several paintings, bunched together, leaned against
the counter on the other side of the worktable.
Claire Ingram bent over, flipping through them, her
back to the door.

"Claire?" I said softly.

She dropped the paintings and dived for the floor.
Sunlight glinted on metal and I saw a rifle in her
hands. I jumped back, sliding around the door
frame into the outer room, pressed against the wall,
my heart thumping.

"I've got a gun," she said, panic edging her voice.
"Who's out there?"

Should I run, take my chances? If she killed Felix,
if I scared her off last night before she found what

she was looking for. . . . I measured the distance to the front door and knew I'd never make it.

"Take it easy. It's Delilah West." I stepped around the doorway, keeping my hands in sight. She crouched behind the table, the rifle trained on the door. Don't let her know you suspect anything, I told myself, and said, "That was a damn fool thing to do. What if it had been one of Bell's men instead of me? You could've got yourself shot."

"I talked to John. I knew they wouldn't be back for a while. After what happened to Felix, I certainly wasn't going to come out here unarmed."

I looked at the rifle and remembered Felix's bloody body. Maybe his death had nothing to do with Janet after all. Maybe it was an act of desperation.

She *looked* desperate enough. Makeup only intensified her pallor. It was like a painted mask separate from the sunburned skin. Tension drew lines around her mouth and across her forehead. The reddish brown eyes were furtive and hunted behind a fringe of mascara. She looked so much like Bak's cruel painting, it gave me a cold shiver.

"What are you doing here?" she demanded, the gun still lined up on my stomach.

"Put the gun down and we'll talk about it," I said quietly.

"What? Oh." She looked down at the rifle as though she'd forgotten it was there and then back at me. A sly grin lifted the corners of her mouth. "What's the matter, Delilah? Scared?"

She put on the safety and laid the gun on the table. I let out a shaky gust of pent-up air. "I've already been the target of one shooting," I said. "Damn right I'm scared."

"Then why did you come back? Seems to me this is the last place you'd want to be."

"I was looking for you. Why don't we get out of here? Let's find someplace private and a few degrees cooler."

"I can't go just yet." Her eyes darted around the room then swung back to me with growing suspicion. "How did you know where to find me?"

"I figured you were looking for something," I said. "It's not here, Claire. I found it last night."

"You found—" She broke off, grabbed for the gun, but I was quicker.

I snatched it up, faced her across the table. Frustration and fear twisted her face. She breathed in shallow gulps.

"Stay there," I said. "Don't move."

"Please, I didn't mean . . . ." She made an obvious effort to control herself. "If you saw that painting, you know why I came here. Just now, I thought maybe I could force you to give it to me, but I wouldn't hurt you. I'd never hurt anybody."

"How about Felix?" I asked. "I wonder what a ballistics check on this rifle would show."

"You don't think that I—no. God, no. He was a sadistic monster and I'll admit I thought about killing him a few times, but I didn't have the nerve to actually do it. Take the rifle if you want. Run tests. It won't prove anything. And while you're at it, you'd better check out a lot of other people. Philip has a gun. We used to go skeet shooting every weekend. And Greg was on the rifle team in college. That's just for starters. Half the people in this town keep weapons."

"But Felix never did one of his special paintings of them. He was blackmailing you, wasn't he?"

"Why, no. Of course not. Why would you assume a thing like that?"

"Yours wasn't the only one." I nodded toward the cupboard where he had stored the paintings. "They're really very good in a twisted sort of way. I imagine he could have sold them. God knows there's a ready market for perversion. But he didn't. He didn't even display them. They were worth more locked up. It's easy enough to guess why."

"All right." Anger mottled her face. "He sure as hell couldn't live on the money he made from this abstract garbage. So I paid him. Not much; he wasn't really greedy. I think he liked the feeling of power over me as much as the money. God knows I'd have paid a lot more. He threatened to show that filthy picture to Philip. You know how Philip hated Felix. If he found out I'd had an affair with him. . . ." She trailed off and looked at me with a calculating stare. "You're taking up where Felix left off, aren't you?"

"You think I'm going to blackmail you?"

"Don't play games, Delilah. Just tell me how much it's going to cost."

"Nothing. Not a goddamn thing. You can have the painting free and clear. But not just yet. I'm going to hang on to it for a while in case it can tie you to Felix's death."

"But I told you I didn't do it," she said. "Check out the rifle."

"Oh, I don't think this is the murder weapon." I levered out the bullets, dropped them into my purse, slid the empty gun across the table to her. "I doubt you'd be stupid enough to be walking around with it. But as you pointed out, it's not the only gun in town.''

"And I'm not the only one who had a reason to get rid of Felix. How about all those other paintings? One was of Janet. I've seen it. Maybe he was blackmailing her, too. If so, she had as good a reason as I did for wanting him dead. Maybe her disappearing act was just to buy her an alibi.''

I tried not to let her see how badly her words had jolted me, but she gave me her ferretlike grin. "John Bell thinks Felix was shot during a robbery. Maybe you'd better leave well enough alone, Delilah. Anyway, he's not going to like it very much if you try to take over the investigation. He's a territorial man and he can be damned ruthless. Assuming, of course, he finds out what you're doing.''

"Careful," I warned. "You're in no position to make threats. Put me in a corner and I'll turn that picture over to Bell. *Your* picture. He'll only have your word that there was one of Janet.''

"You don't classify yourself with Felix, but what do you call that?'' she asked scornfully, picking up the rifle and circling to the door. She brushed past me and turned to add, "You may not be asking for money, but it's still blackmail. You're no better than he was.''

I opened my mouth to counter her words, but she crossed the room in a rush and slammed the front door behind her.

"Damn," I said, anger knotting my hands into fists.

Was she right? What the hell did it matter if she was? I was doing my job, a very nasty job that was not going to get done by being sweet and kind.

Still, her words left me with a sick feeling. Or

maybe it was the house. Suddenly I had to get out of there. I opened the front door just as the Datsun roared to life and took off, trailing dust.

I went outside to my car, fighting to regain some modicum of professional detachment. I was doing pretty well until I noticed a mound of dirt under a mesquite bush a few feet away. I walked over slowly, sank down on my knees beside it, reached out to touch the freshly turned soil.

Goodbyes come hard for me. Even for a mangy dog who was not very appealing and only accidentally saved my life.

It took a while before I could whisper, "Thanks, mutt," and begin the long, hot drive back to town.

13

IT WAS BAD ENOUGH steering the chuck-holed obstacle course with two good hands, but the Darvon was wearing off and I had to keep my left arm as still as possible. Movement started a pulsing pain that radiated up my shoulder and down to my elbow.

I thought briefly about nerve damage and gangrene. Scenes from old movies played through my mind about limbs being sawed off with only whiskey for anesthetic. I wondered how I would look with a hook for a hand. It could be worse. I could have ended up like Felix.

After my meeting with him the day before, I could understand why there were plenty of people who wanted him dead. But if the same person was also responsible for Emmy's death, it limited the suspects considerably. Except for Claire, all those unknown women in Felix's sadistic portrait galley could be eliminated. And surely Janet was not a suspect, despite what Claire said. Emmy was Janet's friend. Not that friendship is a guarantee against murder, but something in my mind kept going back to the fact that Janet and Emmy had known each other before Janet came to Oro. Maybe it was the secrecy that bothered me. It seemed to be the most natural thing in the world to mention their friendship to other people. Yet Janet hadn't talked about it. Neither had Emmy, not even to her son. At least that's what he wanted me to believe.

The Pinto made the bumpy transition from dirt to asphalt and within minutes I was on the edge of town, passing the Adams's house. A car was parked out front. I stopped, backed up, pulled into the driveway.

A sprinkler whirled a thin spray of water on the parched grass. A little late, I thought as I avoided the mist and climbed the cement stoop to ring the bell.

Greg opened the door, his face hardening as he saw me. I wished that, just once, he would look at me without hostility icing his eyes. He was dressed in jeans and a thin cotton T-shirt with a faded U.C.L.A. emblem. Ash blond hair glinted with golden highlights and his tanned skin had a reddish glow as if he'd just spent several hours in the sun. Behind him I could see a large packing box sitting in the middle of the living room.

"I know I'm interrupting," I said. "I apologize. But I need to talk to you."

He nodded curtly and stepped back. "All right. Come on in and let's get it over with."

"I wouldn't dream of imposing on your hospitality," I said with exaggerated politeness, "but I really need a drink of water."

He said nothing, just led the way to the kitchen and filled a glass while I clumsily shook pain pills from the bottle.

"You do like to push yourself to the limit," he observed as I swallowed the pills. "John said you were wounded last night."

"Good old John," I said. "No wonder you don't

have a daily paper in this town. You don't need one. You've got your own town crier.''

"I have an interest in what happened last night. Mesquite Canyon is my property.''

"Now that Emmy is dead," I murmured.

"That's right," he said coldly. "I suppose you're out making up a list of suspects. You may as well put my name on the top. I inherited everything from Emmy. She owned quite a bit of land around town, and there's a fairly large insurance policy with me as the beneficiary. Money's always a motive, isn't it?''

"Yes, it is. Where were you that afternoon when she died?''

"None of your damn business," he said, "but I'll save you a call. I wasn't in my office. And I sure as hell wasn't here. Of course, you only have my word for that.''

"Of course." I held out the glass.

He took it, brushing my fingers with his. I held the contact a second longer than necessary, had to force myself to let go. Jack talked me into sky-diving one time—Jack talked me into a lot of things. My stomach felt like that now—the first breathless moment of free-fall as you tumble straight for earth.

He stared at me, still and watchful, but somehow the hostility was gone. "Funny how the sparks fly when we're together," he said.

"Isn't it?" My mouth was dry. I wished I had the glass back, but I wasn't sure it was because I was thirsty.

"We could call a truce," he said. "At least long enough for coffee. There's a pot already made. Are you game?''

I nodded agreement and he pulled out a chair.
"Sit down. How do you like it?"

"Black's fine."

He filled cups from an electric percolator and put
them on the table. "Are you hungry? It's early, but
how about some lunch?"

"Well," I said, ready to say no, but suddenly
realizing that I was ravenous. "Okay. Can I help?"

"No. It'll just be a sandwich. Nothing fancy.
Drink your coffee."

I watched him take out cheese, slice tomatoes,
butter bread, holding the knife with deft square-
tipped fingers. He reached for plates and shoulder
muscles rippled under the thin shirt. I liked being
there in that kitchen with him. I liked it a lot. Hard
little knots of tension that I'd carried around for
months began to uncurl and a protective circle of
intimacy closed off the grimness of the past few
days. I even forgot about finding Emmy uncon-
scious here on the kitchen floor.

"Want some olives?" he asked, putting the sandwich in front of me. "I think there's a jar in the
refrigerator."

"No, thanks," I said. "I can't stand them."

"We should have called this truce sooner. Look at
all I'm finding out about you. You take your coffee
black and you hate olives. How do you feel about
horses? Do you ride?"

"Not if I can help it," I said. "Did Janet like to go
riding?"

"She loves it. We—" He broke off and shook his
head. "No fair sneaking in questions when the
white flag is out."

"You want to limit the conversation to our tastes
in food?"

"Not at all. Actually, I'd like to know more about you, Delilah." He gave me a long speculative look that sent a frisson of excitement up my spine. "I'm curious. Why did you become a private detective?"

"I married one. Before that, I was in the L.A. police department for a while. It was a few years ago before lady cops got to do much besides being either a glorified secretary or a meter maid. Jack— Jack was my husband—Jack thought we'd make a good team. We did."

"Did. Past tense?"

"Yes. He's dead."

"But you stayed in the business. Why?"

"I wonder myself sometimes. Look, I'll give you my life story very quickly. I'm an only child. My mother died when I was five. My father was a cop until he had a massive cerebral hemorrhage while I was still in college. So I'm an orphan and a widow."

"It's a funny thing about you, Delilah. You measure everything in terms of death."

"Sorry. I forgot my measuring cup." Suddenly I wasn't so sure I liked his probing gaze. "Any more coffee in that pot?"

After he refilled my cup, I said, "All right. Play fair. It's your turn to tell me about yourself. Did you always live in Oro?"

"No. I grew up in the Bay area. Oakland. Walnut Creek. We moved here when dad and Emmy—" He stopped, staring at me over the rim of his cup for a moment before he shrugged, picked up the other half of his sandwich, chewed a moment before he went on. "You're going to find out about this eventually, so I may as well tell you. Emmy was my stepmother. She and my father were married in 1965."

"That's when you came here? Why Oro?"

"I don't know. A fresh start, I guess. Emmy had a little money and property was cheap. Anyway, my mother had died of cancer a couple of years earlier and my dad really wanted to get away."

"Was Emmy from Oakland, too?"

He shook his head and licked a drop of tomato juice from his fingers. "No. Oregon. Dad met her on vacation."

"Beautiful part of the country," I said. "Yet they moved here. Why?"

"You question everything, don't you? It sounds as though the truce is over."

"I guess it is." I pushed away the empty plate and cup. "Did she talk much about her past?"

"Never."

"So it's entirely possible that she's known Janet for years."

"Look, I may only be Emmy's stepson. But she was a mother to me for half my life. During all that time, she never once mentioned Janet Valek."

"Still, she did know her. The birthday card proves that."

"Your deduction. And you are the expert."

"Yes," I said evenly. "I am."

"Well, then, I bow to your superior judgment. If the interview is over, I'll clean up here and get back to my job." He picked up the dishes, made lots of clattering noises as he put them in the sink.

"It's not quite over," I said. "I'm sure Bell told you that Felix was the victim of an armed robbery. I don't buy it anymore than I believe your mother accidentally killed herself. It's all related somehow."

"You never give up, do you? Don't you get exhausted from building all those mountains of logic from such flimsy molehills?"

His words hurt more than I cared to admit. "Look," I said. "You're an accountant. You can read ledgers and financial statements and spot inconsistencies. I do the same thing with people. Something's wrong here. I don't know what it is yet, but I plan to find out."

"Good for you. Let's see, I believe your next question is about my alibi for last night."

"Do you have one?"

"Not unless a horse can testify in court. Now that really does end this conversation, Delilah. I've got an unpleasant afternoon ahead of me sorting out Emmy's things and I'd like to get it over with as quickly as possible."

He strode down the narrow hall and threw open the front door. Stood there, waiting for me to leave. I went reluctantly, dozens of unanswered questions churning in my head. But it was useless to ask them. His face was stony and cold. The truce was definitely over.

Outside the sprinkler was still running. I trudged across soggy grass to my car. As I opened the door and got in, I bumped my shoulder against the window molding. The stab of pain reminded me that I was supposed to go have the bandage changed. I drove over to Dr. Jessup's office and stared at old *National Geographics* until he came back from lunch.

He did a quick job that hurt miserably, looked at the shadows under my eyes and sternly advised me to get a couple of hours of sleep.

It sounded like a good idea so I went back to the motel. When I let myself into the room, the message light was burning on the telephone. The office told me that Rita Braddock had called several times and that Lawrence Valek wanted to talk to me immediately. I didn't want to talk to him—or to Rita. They'd ask what I was doing to trace Janet and the truth was I hadn't done a thing. All I had to report was another murder and my deepening suspicion that Janet would never be found alive.

I told the office that I didn't want to be disturbed, pulled down the shades, took another pill. Then I lay down on the rock-hard bed in the semidarkness. Tossed restlessly. Thought about Greg and how much I wished he was sharing the bed with me.

Great, I thought. Just what I need. Nothing like lust to muddy my thinking.

Like it or not, Greg was as much a suspect as Claire and Philip. More so, maybe. He was hiding things from me, using sex appeal and personal attacks to throw me off. But he knew Janet a lot better than he wanted me to believe. I knew it with the instinct of a jealous woman. And who had a better opportunity to get to Emmy or to Felix?

The key to the whole thing was the motive. Once I knew why, the who would be easy. I reached for the telephone.

The Los Angeles number I dialed connected me with the Colfax Agency. After running the gamut of receptionists and secretaries, I finally got through to the man who ran it. Charlie Colfax and Jack went a long way back. They met in Vietnam when the war was still a police action. Afterward they were partners for a while. It didn't last. Charlie wanted to have the biggest agency in the business, complete with computers, luxurious offices and cold-eyed accountants. He hasn't succeeded, but he's come pretty damn close.

After Jack died, Charlie offered me a job. "Good

salary, regular hours," he said. "Standing offer."
Maybe he felt he owed it to Jack for old debts I
don't know about. I didn't take him up on it. Instead, I let him pay it off on the installment plan.
Like now.

Charlie isn't much for formalities so we got them
over quickly and I gave him what I had on Emmy
Adams and asked for a background check.

"I'm particularly interested in any connection
with a woman named Janet Valek."

"Any relation to Valek Construction?"

"Lawrence Valek's daughter," I told him, wondering why he bothers with computers. "This may
go back a way."

"Immaterial. I'll go back as far as necessary.
Anything else?"

"Mrs. Adams's stepson, Greg. And the partners in
a real-estate company here in Oro, El Rancho Realty. Claire Ingram and Philip Hunter."

He asked a few questions and I gave him all
the background material I had on my suspects.
"This Adams woman," he said finally. "You say
she's dead. Are you getting in over your head,
Delilah?"

"Probably, but I know how to swim."

He sighed. "You and Jack were a matched pair,
both stubborn mules. Okay, okay, I'm minding my
own business. I'll get back to you."

I gave him my telephone number and hung up.
The call had taken a little of the pressure off. I lay
back down and let my mind, awash with Darvon,
float pleasantly. Sleep seemed a real possibility until somebody knocked on the door.

"Go 'way," I mumbled.

Another knock, louder this time.

"Who is it?" I shouted over the drone of the air conditioner. "What do you want?"

"Sheriff's department. Open up."

The tone of the voice suggested that I'd better comply or the door would be kicked in. I stumbled over and opened it a few inches. The officer who stood outside was the size of Muhammad Ali and had the jawline of a pit bulldog.

"Delilah West? Sheriff Bell wants to see you in his office. Now."

"Am I under arrest?"

He smiled. It was the kind of smile you'd expect after he'd just kicked his mother down a flight of stairs. "Bell said to bring you in. He didn't say how. You want to do it the hard way?"

14

I SUGGESTED FOLLOWING HIM to the station in my own car, but he gave me another smile, tucked his ham-sized hand under my elbow and steered me to the black and white. As we skimmed through town I got to stare at the back of his pitted neck through the wire mesh screen that separated the back seat from the driver. At least he didn't pat me down for weapons or take me in handcuffs.

Still, it seemed like Bell was coming down pretty hard just for delaying a lousy statement. By the time we swung into the parking lot at the substation, I was trying to keep a lid on my temper. The s.o.b. might not have the right to treat me this way, but he had the power to do what he pleased. In the exercise of that power, he had me trapped and helpless and I was sure he knew it.

There were no handles on the inside of the door, so I had to wait for Smiley to let me out. He grabbed my arm and marched me inside.

"You can let go now," I told him. "If I try to run, you can always shoot me in the leg."

He gave me another look at his teeth and escorted me past the front desk, down the hall to Bell's door where he knocked and stuck his head inside to announce, "I got the West dame."

"Bring her in," Bell said. "Tell Angie to get ready

to take a statement. I'll give her a buzz as soon as Delilah and I have a little talk.''

So now we were on a first-name basis. It ought to have sounded nice and cozy, but it didn't.

Smiley said, ''Right,'' unclamped his fingers from my arm and left us alone.

Bell glowered at me across his desk. Anger hardened and angled his face, but he was working hard to keep his temper under control.

''Have a seat,'' he said tightly.

''You could've called,'' I said. ''You didn't have to haul me in like a criminal.''

''If you'd come in like I requested, it wouldn't have been necessary.''

''I was under doctor's orders to rest.''

''Let's stop playing games, Delilah. You were supposed to be here first thing this morning, but instead you were running around questioning people. We're going to talk about it, so sit down.'' This time it was an order, crackling through the air like thunder.

I sat. I was close enough to see a vein throbbing in his temple and a twitch in one eyelid.

''I warned you about overstepping boundaries,'' he said. ''That P.I. ticket of yours does not give you the authority to investigate a murder.''

''It does allow me to look for a missing person. That's what I'm doing. I'm only investigating aspects of the murder that have a connection with the disappearance of Janet Valek.''

''And if there aren't any, why, you'll just make some up. I'll tell you again. It's my jurisdiction, my case. You make a statement today and that's the end of it. Ask one more question, bother one more person in this town, and I'll shovel so much crap over you, it'll take six months to dig your way out. Understand me?"

"Oh, yes," I said. "It's also clear that somebody's been complaining. Claire Ingram didn't waste any time, did she?"

"Claire? You been bothering her, too?"

So it was Greg, I thought bitterly. He'd warned me, but somehow I hadn't believed he'd go this far.

"Look, sheriff," I said, making a supreme effort to hit a conciliatory tone. "Can't we work together on this? Felix Bak was your all-around louse and there are a lot of people who would've liked to see him dead. It seems to me—"

"No!" he roared, and thumped his fist on the desk. "You got any evidence, I want it now. Then pack your bags and get the hell out of town. Is that clear enough?"

"Succinctly put," I said. "You won't mind if I check with my doctor, will you? He did recommend bed rest."

"You have an hour from the time you sign your statement. After that you can rest in jail."

"On what charge?"

"Impeding an officer in the pursuit of his duties will do for starters. If I find out you're holding something back, I'll add obstructing justice and then I'll really start digging." He hit the intercom button and barked, "Angie. Ready for you now."

It didn't take long for the stenographer's experienced fingers to take down my statement. Bell saw to it that I kept it brief and to the point. I came, I saw, I got shot in the arm. No sense telling him about the portraits or any of my other theories. He was looking for an excuse to throw me in jail. Damned if I'd gift wrap it for him.

When Angie tapped out the final sentence, I was banished to the outer office to wait for the statement to be prepared. I sat on a hard wooden bench and listened to her machine-gun typing firing away in the next room. Counted the holes in the porous tile on the floor. Read all the printed information thumbtacked to the bulletin board.

There were duty rosters. Plans for the annual department picnic. The poster for the open house held last night. Pardners in Keeping the Peace, it said. Oh, sure. Just try to help, fella. See what happens.

I wandered restlessly over to the water cooler with the duty officer watching my every move. My eyes kept going back to the poster. Something about that open house stirred a response in a corner of my mind. I drank some water, tried to make the connection that would call up the memory that felt like an itch just beyond the reach of scratching fingernails.

Damn. Dropping the paper cup into the wastebasket, I walked back to my chair, unable to remember what it was. The man on the desk still watched me. He was about half the size of Smiley, with carefully combed limp brown hair, prominent eyes, a mustache that tried to balance a weak chin. I stopped at the desk, gave him a smile and nodded toward the poster.

"How'd it go?"

"What? The open house? Okay," he admitted warily, crushing out a cigarette.

"Were you on duty, Officer. . .Officer Kemp?" I read his name off a plastic sign.

"Everybody was. We all pulled an extra shift." There was a slight edge of injury in his voice.

"I'll bet you're exhausted," I said, purring sympathy. I perched on the edge of the desk, making sure my dress hiked up to show my kneecap. "A double shift yesterday and back at work again today—my goodness, I don't know how you do it."

He expanded to his full five feet eight inches and said, "That's nothing. Why, last winter when it flooded over at Lake Elsinore—"

"Wasn't that something?" I cut in, fiddling with the button on my dress and watching his Adam's apple bob up and down. "Of course the open house wasn't that kind of emergency, but still I heard you were awfully busy."

It occurred to me I had heard it. From Philip, I recalled, when we talked on the telephone. "Just about everybody in town is there," he had said. The trickle of excitement turned to a full-scale avalanche as I remembered the rest of that conversation.

". . . and I never did figure out why we had such a crowd," Kemp was saying.

"I think it shows what a good relationship you have with the public," I said, widening my eyes in earnest admiration. "I can see you have a lot of empathy with people."

"Yeah? Well, I do my best. I mean, community relations is a big part of my job. Our job," he amended generously.

"You must be doing something right. Look at the turnout. Somebody told me that even Felix Bak came by."

"Come to think of it, he *was* here," Kemp said.

"Well, there you are. If you can get somebody like Bak to drop in—not to speak ill of the dead, but we both know he wasn't exactly your average law-abiding citizen." Careful, I told myself. I wanted to scream, what the hell was he *doing* here? But I forced myself to keep up the casual flow of innocuous questions. "Did you open up everything to the public?"

"Just about. There was a tour of the facilities, including a look at the police cars. That's always a big hit with the kids. I ran license plates. People are fascinated with the way the computer knows all about their driving record. Except we turned up an unpaid parking ticket on one guy. He didn't think it was so great."

"Sounds like Bak," I said, trying to steer the man's memory back to the subject.

"No, but that was another funny thing."

I felt like screaming in frustration as he paused to light a cigarette and slowly dragged in smoke.

"What?" I prompted.

"Well, it was a little embarrassing, because Bak gave me his plate to run, and it turned out to be registered to somebody else. Of course when I checked, he said he'd mixed up the number sequence, which explained the mistake."

"Maybe it wasn't a mistake," I said carefully. "Knowing Bak, he probably had a few a.k.a.'s floating around."

"Not this one, believe me. It belonged to that state senator, Hodge. Remember him? The one from Orange County who went to jail a while back."

"Oh, yeah," I said vaguely, trying to hide my confusion by leaving my perch on his desk and going over to the water cooler.

Hodge, I thought with disbelief. What the hell?

It was like working on a jigsaw puzzle and knowing a piece was lost. Then somebody hands it to you, but you still don't have the faintest idea where it belongs. It fit. I was sure of it. Felix hadn't just accidentally wandered into the open house and come up with that license number. It was about as likely as a fox wandering into a pack of hound dogs. No, he'd seen the number somewhere and remembered it.

Not such a difficult feat, I decided as I thought about the big black Lincoln parked on Lawrence Valek's driveway. Both the letters and numbers on the plate had been arranged in alphabetic and numerical sequence. If it stuck in my mind, Felix, with his artist's eye for detail, was sure to have remembered it.

"Mrs. West?" Kemp said sharply.

"Sorry," I said, turning around. The girl had joined him, a sheaf of typed papers in her hand. I widened my apologetic smile to include both of them. "I had a pretty exhausting night myself so I'm kind of out of it. What did you say?"

"Angie's finished with the statement. You want to come over and sign it? The copies, too. Better read it first."

"I'm sure it's perfectly accurate," I said, scribbling my name and enduring the pressure of his leg against mine.

"I need a ride back to my motel," I said.

I didn't mean it as an invitation, but he took it for one.

He brushed a careless hand against my breast as he reached for the papers and said, "Just let me check with Sheriff Bell. I'll see if I can get away."

Oh, Christ, I groaned inwardly, visualizing a wrestling match when we got back to my room. But he came back with a scowl on his face and Smiley close on his heels.

"Let's go," Smiley said as he latched onto my arm.

I let him march me out to the patrol car and settled down with a sigh of relief for the short ride. When we parked in front of my room, Smiley opened the door and stood there while I got out and fumbled in my purse for the key.

"Don't let me keep you," I said.

"Don't worry, you're not." He gave me his icy grin. "I'm on my lunch break. I'm going to eat right here at the café. I figure it'll take me an hour and then I'll come back and help you with your bags."

Good old Bell, I thought. He's really a man of his word.

"Bon appetit," I told Smiley as he gave me a two-finger salute and ambled over to the café. I only hoped he tried one of their hamburgers.

I let myself into the refrigerated little cave of my room and sat down on the bed. Packing would be easy. I'd never unpacked so all I had to do was close up my suitcase. I had an hour before I would be evicted. An hour to make some sense of what I'd learned.

I knew now what Felix had remembered. The only thing I had to figure out was what the hell it meant.

15

THERE WAS ONLY ONE LOGICAL REASON why Felix would run Daniel Hodge's license plate through the police computer. He'd seen the black Lincoln parked in front of Janet's house the night she disappeared.

I sat on the edge of the bed in the dimly lighted room and tried to piece together what I knew about that night. According to Philip, Janet turned down a dinner invitation because she was tired and wanted to go to bed early. It sounded like an excuse she would use if she really was going to be busy with somebody else.

But who? Felix? Or Daniel Hodge?

Two different scenarios came to mind. One: Felix's hazy memory of plans for a dinner date with Janet was correct. While she waited for him, Hodge dropped in. His car was there when Felix, fuzzy-headed with dope and art, drove into town. Maybe his brain cleared for a minute and he remembered his plans with Janet. He stopped, but another car was there on the driveway so he drove off, thinking he'd made a mistake.

The second set of possibilities was really only a minor variation of the first. Felix didn't have a date with Janet that night. Confusion seemed his natural state of mind. He could easily have made a mistake.

The end result was the same however. He stopped and saw Hodge's car.

My questions had jogged his memory and he managed to find out through a clever bit of subterfuge who owned the black Lincoln.

I got up and paced restlessly around the room. How did Hodge know where to find Janet and why did he come here? Hodge and Lawrence Valek had been friends and business associates for years, but according to David, Janet didn't like Hodge. I remembered the sick old man I'd met that day in Valek's study. He'd been here in Oro, seen Janet. Did Valek know that? Had they let me flounder around here, stringing together all kinds of crazy conclusions when they both knew exactly what had happened to her?

They've taken her away, I thought. She flipped out on drugs, or she's alcoholic and they've put her someplace to dry out.

In that case Bell was right about Emmy and Felix. The old woman's death was an accident and a known drug user was killed by somebody looking for a quick high.

Good old Delilah, getting gassed and shot at and ordered out of town. And for what? Nothing, I thought bitterly as I gathered up toiletries and threw them into my suitcase. Slammed the lid shut.

The action started a throb of pain in my arm. I went into the bathroom for a glass of water, brought it back and set it on the night table while I dug out the bottle of Darvon. After I swallowed a pill, I wadded two pillows against the headboard and leaned against them, waiting for the medication to take effect.

Valek's going to pay for this, I promised myself,

shivering as the memory of last night in Mesquite Canyon washed over me.

So much death. I could still smell it, taste it, feel it run in cold rivers of fear through my bloodstream.

I remembered and I knew what had happened out there. Murder. The conviction was stronger than ever. The same day I came to Oro asking questions about Janet, Emmy was killed. Felix remembered something about the night Janet disappeared. Assume it was Hodge's car. A few hours after he identified it, he was dead.

Maybe Valek didn't know about Hodge's visit to his daughter. Maybe only one man knew. Hodge.

I swung my legs over the side of the bed, ready to grab my suitcase and leave, but the telephone rang. I picked it up and said a distracted, "Hello?"

"Hello yourself," Rita said. "I suppose you've got a good reason for ignoring my calls and for not checking in."

"Sorry," I said. "Things have been happening pretty fast out here. As a matter of fact, I was just on my way out, Rita, so—"

"What things? Delilah—"

"Fill you in later," I said and hung up.

I reached for my suitcase and the phone shrilled again. "Damn," I said as I picked it up. "Now, listen, Rita—"

"Delilah? It's Charlie Colfax. I've got that information you wanted."

"Information?" My head was full of so many things for a moment I forgot what I had asked him.

"If you don't need it—"

"No, no. That's okay, Charlie. Go ahead."

He gave me a brief personal rundown on Philip and Claire that checked with Philip's story. "About their business," he went on. "El Rancho Realty is in big trouble. Tight money and the gasoline situation have about done them in. Some notes are coming due soon. The whole operation is ready to fold."

"I thought so, but they put up a good front," I said, wondering how much they owed on their expensive cars and fancy offices. "What else have you got?"

"Let's see. Greg Adams. Drafted into the Army and served in Vietnam. When he got out, he went to U.C.L.A. for his degree in accounting. Worked for a big firm in Riverside until he passed his C.P.A. exams, then he moved back to Oro and set up his own business."

"Is he having financial problems?" I asked.

"Has a pretty heavy mortgage on some property outside of town and some college loans still outstanding, but he ought to be in good shape now. There was a hundred thousand dollar insurance policy on his stepmother. Double indemnity."

No wonder he wants Emmy's death to be an accident, I thought grimly. "What about his stepmother?" I asked. "What did you find out about her?"

"The information's sketchy but I did find out she was born in Coos Bay, Oregon. Dates of her marriage to Thomas Adams and her move to Oro check with what you gave me. Now, the Valeks are something else again. Lots of information on them, and I found the connection to Mrs. Adams. Janet's mother was born in the same town, Coos Bay, Oregon."

"They were probably friends," I said. "And Janet kept in touch after her mother died."

"Very likely, I'd say. Also she might have become

pretty close to the Adams woman around the time her brother, David, was born.''

"You'll have to explain that.''

"When we did a routine check on the Valeks I found out that the boy was also born in Coos Bay. I got curious so we dug up some newspaper stories. Valek was moving up just then, so his son's birth rated a mention in one of the local papers' social column. Seems Janet and her mother were visiting in Oregon while Mrs. Valek was pregnant. She took a fall that caused some complications and she couldn't be moved until after David was born. So an old friend might have helped out.''

"Makes sense,'' I agreed, and it did. But it didn't explain why Lawrence Valek would deny knowing about Emmy.

A loud thump sounded on the thin panel of the motel door. Smiley. My hour must be up. I covered the mouthpiece and shouted, "Just a minute,'' then I spoke urgently into the phone. "Listen, Charlie, I didn't think about this earlier, but maybe you came across something about Valek and Daniel Hodge. Do you know who he is?''

"Sure. I've heard the name. I know he and Valek are supposed to have pulled some slick maneuvers with state funds, but it was Hodge who got caught. There's tons of stuff about them, Delilah. What exactly do you want?''

"I don't know,'' I said helplessly, and then seized on the only thing that came to mind. "How about the highway construction down in this area? Has Valek got any connection with the Interstate that's going in?''

"Doesn't sound like his kind of job, but of course I

wasn't looking specifically for that information. Do you want me to check it out for you?''

More pounding. ''Mrs. West?'' Smiley yelled. ''Time's up. Open the door.''

''I'm coming. Charlie,'' I said rapidly, ''see what you can find. And listen, I know you've got a copy of every kind of directory in print. Can you get me Daniel Hodge's home address?''

''You mean right now?''

''Please.''

''Okay. Hang on.''

There was a deadening click as he put me on hold. I laid down the phone and padded over to the door. ''I just got out of the shower,'' I said loudly. ''I'm getting dressed. It won't take a minute. Okay?''

He muttered something about hurrying it up and I went back to the phone. A few seconds later Charlie came on to give me an address in what had once been an exclusive area of Anaheim.

''Thanks, Charlie,'' I said and hung up.

Grabbing my purse and suitcase, I went to open the door. Smiley stood there, sweating steadily in the midday heat.

''You can tell Bell I'm on my way,'' I said, walking briskly over to my car. Just in time, I remembered the paintings still in the trunk so I put the suitcase in the back seat. ''No need for you to wait around,'' I told him. ''I'll check out and be on my way.''

''I've got nothing else to do.''

To prove it he folded his arms across his massive chest and leaned against the patrol car. He was still standing there when I got back from paying the bill at the motel office. As I drove away, he climbed into his car and followed me for several miles until I got on the Interstate. Only then did he head back for town.

As I drove north, gusts of hot air whipped my hair into my eyes. Brush fires were still burning in several locations. Smoke combined with ozone and exhaust fumes to turn the air into an environmentalist's nightmare, a kind of chemical soup that stung the eyes and burned the lungs.

Pain stabbed behind my eyes and in my temples as the completed section of I-15 ended abruptly and I followed Route 71 past dusty orange groves into the dry, barren hills of Corona where it joined the Riverside Freeway. I couldn't tell if it was from the pollution or the bewildering mass of information I was trying to assimilate.

After my talk with Charlie, I knew that I'd been right about Janet and Emmy. I'd wondered before why Janet didn't leave her father's house and make a life of her own. Maybe she had, finally. She saw a chance to come to Oro, to a place where she had a friend. Felix might have been an excuse, a blind. Her father would understand Felix. Then something happened. Something connected with Hodge.

Did it follow that Hodge was responsible for the deaths of Emmy and Felix? One thing was for sure. That sick old man in Valek's study did not lay down a deadly barrage of sniper fire and then run through the moonless darkness to a car parked somewhere outside Mesquite Canyon. He was not physically capable of it.

But he has money, I thought grimly as I hit the Orange Freeway interchange and headed south. And there are always guns for hire.

Of course I might find out that Hodge was not directly involved, that he was merely the last person to see Janet that night. In any case, I wanted to know why he hadn't told me about it.

I got off the freeway in Anaheim and crawled along surface streets that were beginning to back up with early rush-hour traffic. Hodge lived a block away from the busy commercial district on a street that seemed to hold time and progress at bay. Here, huge old houses sat in the middle of spacious lawns shaded by tall magnolias. Banks of shrubbery and flowering vines marked property boundaries. An occasional overgrown fan palm thrust bulging trunks against the sidewalk. It was the kind of neighborhood that had become an anachronism in the high-priced, land-hungry Orange County economy.

Hodge lived in the middle of the block in a two-storied mansion that looked transplanted either from the deep south or M.G.M.'s back lot. I parked on a sweeping arc of driveway and walked up to the porticoed entrance, lifted a heavy brass knocker that was the tongue in the mouth of a roaring lion.

I expected a servant dressed for the part, but the door was opened by a tall, elegantly dressed woman with anxious eyes. Her face was the type that was pleasantly pretty in youth but grew more distinctive with the passage of time. Dark hair, streaked with silver, was swept back to reveal skin still taut over high cheekbones. In the gloomy cavern of the entryway, her face looked ashy gray, shadowed along the bony eye sockets.

"Mrs. Hodge?" I guessed.

"I was expecting someone else. I'm sorry." She pushed the door, but I caught it, held it open. "I can't talk to anyone right now," she said. "You'll have to come back some other time."

"I want to see your husband. Tell him it's Delilah West." I slipped inside and she backed away, one hand moving up to her throat.

"Please, you have to leave him alone." Begging was a painfully new experience and the words came out harsh and stilted. "He's a sick man and all this hounding is making it worse, so please—"

"Emily," Hodge called querulously from a balcony that ran along an upstairs hall. "I thought I heard the door. Is it—" He broke off as he leaned over the carved railing and saw me, his face like a deflated white balloon suspended in the shadowy vestibule.

"Mr. Hodge, I have to talk to you about Janet."

"No, I can't," he said hoarsely. "Not right now. I'm not feeling well."

"You don't have to talk to her, Dan," Emily said. "I'll send her away. Please go back to bed." She turned to me. "You'll have to go look for a story someplace else. I mean it. I'll call the police. We don't have to be harassed by the newspapers like this."

"I'm not a reporter," I said. "Your husband knows me. Ask him."

"Dan?" She raised frightened eyes.

Hodge came down the stairs slowly, hanging on to the railing. She reached for him and he patted her hands, but his eyes never left my face. They were full of old secrets, dark and terrible.

"We have to talk," I repeated. "I think it would be best if we were alone."

Emily gave a fluttering cry of protest, but Hodge nodded. "She's right, Emily. There are... things... we have to discuss. Please, darling. I'm fine. Come up to the library," he said to me.

I followed him up the stairs, down the hallway that ran along the balcony. The library door was open. Inside, leather-covered sofas flanked a fireplace full of ashes. Books lined the walls. The room smelled of ink and calfskin bindings and mildew. Hodge closed the door and sat on one of the sofas facing me, adding a stench of fear to the rest of the odors.

"You knew, didn't you?" he said dully. "I saw it in your eyes that day in Larry's study. You knew that Janet was dead."

16

HIS WORDS CREATED A SHOCK that traveled in a searing wave over my body, leaving me numb and hollow. I'd known it was probably true, expected it, but to hear him say the words. . . .

"She was dead," he repeated, plucking at the narrow lapels of a maroon robe belted around his skinny body. "She just lay there, so still. I didn't mean to hurt her. I'm not very strong and I didn't think—but she fell and . . . I tried to talk to her. I pleaded. It all happened so long ago, but she—"

He broke off as voices sounded in the hall, Emily's high-pitched flutter overlaid by a deep baritone. The door was flung open and Lawrence Valek strode in like a thunderstorm looking for a place to explode. There hadn't been time for Emily to call him just to get rid of me. It was Valek she had been expecting when she opened the door and found me standing there.

"I wanted to send her away," Emily said, "but Dan insisted and so—"

"I'll handle it, Emily. Go on downstairs now."

"Yes, well. . . ." She looked at our faces and backed away, raising her hands as if to shield herself from what she saw.

"Get out of here," Valek said, towering over me.

"Leave right now or I'll make damn sure you never work in this state again."

Sickness and fear rushed in to fill the void in the middle of my chest. Did Valek know? Was he protecting the man who killed his daughter? He was a vicious, unprincipled bastard, but I couldn't believe he was capable of that. And if he didn't know what had happened, the knowledge would be a terrible revelation. Either way, I felt compelled to find out the truth.

"Didn't you hear me?" he roared. "Out. Now."

"I can't leave," I said. "Mr. Hodge and I haven't finished our talk. It was just getting interesting."

He turned on Hodge. "What did you tell her?"

"I didn't have to tell her anything, Larry. She already knows."

"She knows nothing," Valek said contemptuously. "A lot of crazy guesses, that's all."

"I know that Emmy Adams was a friend of your wife's," I said. "They were both from Coos Bay, Oregon. She and Janet kept in touch over the years."

"If you'd done what you promised," Hodge cried, "if you'd kept her away from that woman—I paid, didn't I? Enough money so she could go anywhere."

"I had no idea Emmy was in Oro," Valek said. "And I certainly didn't know that Janet was in contact with her. She always was a sly, deceitful child. But she'll have to give it up now, Dan. Emmy's dead. Without her, Janet can't prove a thing."

He didn't know. Hodge's trapped, imploring eyes confirmed the realization. I knew I should leave, go straight to a telephone, and call the police. Let them handle the explosive situation that was developing here. I couldn't do it. Some part of Janet Valek was in this room, locked up in the secret memories of these two men. I had to know what it was.

I went over to the couch and sat beside Hodge. "Ask Mr. Valek to leave us alone," I said quietly. "We have to finish our conversation, and I really don't think you want him to hear it."

"Don't be ridiculous," Valek snapped. "It's you who are leaving, Mrs. West. Do I have to throw you out bodily? I will, you know."

"I don't think so," I said. "If you do, I'll call the police."

"No," Hodge cried. "Please, you don't understand. Janet—"

"Shut up!" Fury mottled Valek's face. "Don't say anything. Call the police and be damned, Mrs. West. It's none of their affair or yours. It's personal, strictly a family matter."

"Stop it," Hodge said, rubbing his temples with trembling fingers. "I can't think—all this shouting and my head—I can't stand it anymore. It wasn't my fault. I didn't mean to hurt her. I was drunk and—"

"Dan, that's enough." Valek started toward him, but I moved quickly between them.

"She had a crush on me," Hodge went on. His high-pitched voice and the dreamy glaze on his eyes sent a cold chill knifing along my backbone. Valek stood very still and I heard his breath rattle hard in his throat.

"We used to laugh about it, Larry, remember?" Hodge went on. "She always followed me around. That night at the party she followed me down to the beach. Such a beautiful little girl standing there in the moonlight, and she loved me so much. I just went a little crazy, that's all.''

The words trailed off. Huge tears rolled down his face and gobbling sounds came from his mouth as sobs racked the cavernous chest.

I turned away, sickened, and looked at Valek. His face was unreadable, cold and remote, but I understood it just the same.

"My God," I said. "This man, this *friend*, raped your daughter and you did nothing about it."

"What should I have done? Killed him? Had him arrested and create a scandal to ruin all our lives?"

"How about Janet? You've done a pretty good job of destroying hers. She was just a child. She was—" I broke off to make a computation and guessed, "She was thirteen years old. That was the reason she and her mother went to Oregon that summer, wasn't it? Emmy Adams knew what happened to her."

Something flickered behind the smooth surface of his eyes and he nodded. "So now you have your sordid secret, Mrs. West. You can send me a big fat bill, big enough to take you out of your dirty little office and set you up in a high-rise with money to spare."

"Blackmail? The way Hodge paid off Mrs. Adams and the way you milked him all these years?" I looked at the pathetic old man who whimpered on the couch. "All that help you got from your good friend, Senator Hodge, that's what it was. Blackmail."

"No. A friend helping a friend to salvage a terrible situation. And gratitude. Not blackmail."

"You don't even realize what you've done," I said.

"Me? I've just tried to make the best of things for all of us."

"You're as much to blame as he is, and I want you to know it." I dropped down in front of Hodge and grabbed his shoulder. "Mr. Hodge, tell him. Tell him what you told me about Janet."

He shook his head from side to side and tried to pull away. The robe fell open, exposing his chest, bony and hairless like an old chicken plucked clean and eviscerated.

"Leave him alone," Valek said. "He never did get over going to prison. He's already had one heart attack. What are you trying to prove by going on with this?"

"The truth. Since he won't repeat it, I'll tell you myself. Just before you came in here, he told me that Janet was dead."

"What?" Color drained from his face. He backed up to the opposite sofa and sat down, quickly, as though his legs couldn't hold him up. "What are you talking about? Janet—no, I don't believe it."

"He was there in Oro. Ask him."

"Dan?" He leaned forward. Sweat shined his chalky skin. "Dan, I want to know what happened to Janet."

"She threatened to tell Emily if we tried to stop her. She said David had to know the truth. I've paid for it, haven't I, Larry? How could she do that to me? I couldn't stand it if David found out. And Emily—she does love me. I never knew how much. She suffered so much when I went to prison. I won't have her hurt again. I told Janet that, but she wouldn't listen, so I—I had to—"

"My God, what have you done? Why didn't you

come to me? I'd have stopped her, put her away someplace until she came to her senses."

"I thought if I talked to her, pleaded, so I went there...to Oro. But it was useless. She said Emmy would back her up. I was desperate. I didn't mean to hurt her. I grabbed her. She pulled away—fell against the edge of the coffee table. Oh, God, it's all a nightmare. I don't know what to believe anymore. She was dead, she *was*, but...."

"Dan, listen to me. I'll call your attorney. It was an accident, a tragic accident, but you panicked because of your prison record. None of this has to come out, Dan, if you keep your mouth shut."

"I don't believe this," I said, appalled. "He killed your daughter and you're willing to cover it up and make it go away?"

"Mrs. West, please save your self-righteous indignation." Valek was on his feet again and firmly in control. "Yes, I'll clean up this mess the best way I can. I can't help Janet now, but I have to do what's best for David. Anyway, you heard what Dan said. It was an accident. Now I'm going to get a doctor over here and call his attorney."

"No, Larry. Wait." Hodge stretched out a shaking hand. "I keep trying to tell you. She *was* dead. I know she was. He said he'd take care of her. No one would ever know I'd been responsible. I gave him money. I paid. Didn't I pay, Larry?"

He. An accomplice. "Who was it?" I demanded harshly. "Who helped you get rid of Janet's body and killed Mrs. Adams and Felix Bak?"

"Bak?" Valek said. "What the hell are you talking about?"

I ignored him and concentrated on Hodge. His

face was like moist clay, clammy and gray, pulled out of shape by his quivering mouth.

"Look at me," I said. "Tell me his name."

"Emmy knew everything. He said she'd talk. I didn't know until after it...after it happened. Easy, he said. She'd gone blind. I didn't know that. I would have stopped him. I swear I would. But— too late and I was going crazy—the body—nobody found the body. Bak, he said it would be Bak, but then Bak called...and...."

"That's enough for now," Valek said harshly. "I'm going to get an ambulance." He ran from the room and I heard him shouting, "Emily!"

Hodge kept babbling, but it was so incoherent I almost missed the last garbled phrase.

"What did you say?" I shouted, trying to reach him before he slipped away completely. "Answer me, Hodge. Snap out of it."

"Don't remember," he said thickly. "She was dead. I know she was." He looked at me, but his vision had turned inward and saw only horror.

"Dammit," I said. "There was something else. Think. Tell me what it was."

"Unnecessary...all unnecessary. Janet," he whispered, his eyes clear for one final moment. "Janet called me. She's alive."

17

I WAS AFRAID TO BREATHE, afraid the slightest movement would extinguish the dying flicker of lucidity in the old man's eyes.

"Where?" I asked softly. "Where is she?"

"I told him she called...told him...it was over...."

A spasm convulsed his body, arched it off the sofa and onto the floor. His eyes bulged and a rattling noise came from his mouth.

I saw motion from the corner of my eye and looked up. Emily came through the door and screamed, "Dan! Oh, my God!" She ran over and dropped to her knees beside him. "Darling, hold on. The doctor's coming." She cradled his head on her lap and snarled at me, "Get out. Get out and leave us alone."

I stumbled to my feet, filled with a terrible urgency of my own. Ran down the stairs. Valek met me on the bottom step and trapped me there with outstretched arms.

"Get out of my way," I said. "I'm going to find your daughter."

"Janet? What are you talking about? You heard Dan. She's dead."

"We both heard him, but it was only part of the story. He thought he killed Janet. He believed it until she called him a little while ago."

"Called him?"

"She's alive," I said. "I want to make sure she stays that way."

Upstairs in the library, Emily Hodge began to scream. It diverted Valek's attention so I could duck beneath his arm. I went outside, slammed the door behind me, mercifully cutting off the cry that echoed through the house in a grief-filled crescendo.

Find Janet. The single thought filled my mind as I swung the car down the driveway and onto the street. A siren bleated in the distance, its two-note wail growing louder. Too late. Too late for the old man who'd ruined so many lives with a senseless act of violence. Too late for Janet Valek?

Hodge's last words played over and over in my mind. "I told him she'd called."

So his accomplice knew that Janet had spoken with Hodge. Maybe Hodge was too dazed to tell her the connection between them, but would he take a chance on the babblings of that terrified old man and let Janet live?

God knows why he kept her alive in the first place, but I could imagine how it must have happened. He struck a bargain with Hodge and took the body away to dispose of it. Only Janet wasn't dead. I couldn't understand why when he discovered that fact he didn't simply finish the job. Maybe he thought he could have it both ways. Use the situation to play on Hodge's guilt for a while so he could bleed him for money and still have Janet. It worked beautifully. A grateful Janet. A cooperative Hodge. Then I showed up and the simple little blackmail scheme escalated into murder.

Dammit, I thought, all he had to do was have

Janet come back to town. He didn't have to kill Emmy, unless. . . .

A traffic light changed in front of me. I braked hard to miss a Toyota turning left on the yellow. Fishtailed through the intersection to the accompaniment of blaring horns and shouted curses. A sign pointed the way to the Orange Freeway. I could see the entrance ramp clogged with cars and the stop and go crawl of rush-hour traffic on the broad expanse of elevated concrete.

I turned down a side street, staying off the main routes as I plotted a zigzag course to the Riverside Freeway, the only way to get through the northern end of the Santa Ana Mountains and connect with Route 71.

Every traffic light, every snarled intersection, fueled my growing sense of despair. I had to get to Oro. I'd avoided the knowledge long enough. *He*, I kept thinking, but I knew the name. It rose like bile in my throat.

Finish the thought, I told myself savagely. He didn't have to kill Emmy unless. . . unless he had another reason. Like two hundred thousand dollars in life insurance. Say it. Greg. Greg had Janet.

Janet is not dead, he'd told me. No wonder he said it with such emphatic certainty. He knew she was alive.

The sun slid toward the western horizon, still bright enough to strike blinding flashes of light off the glass and chrome of the oncoming traffic. Cars. Millions of cars. A solid barricade of metal. I'd never get to Janet in time.

Christ, what was I doing? Running blindly, all reaction and no brain. Guilt was driving me. A guilt that demanded a personal expiation. If I saved

Janet, somehow it would make up for Emmy and Felix.

Forget it. Get help. Warn Janet.

I headed for a surface street, looking for a phone booth. A lone cubicle with the familiar blue logo sat on the edge of a service-station parking area. The folding door couldn't close out the noise so I pressed the receiver hard against my ear and shouted my request into the mouthpiece.

"Greg Adams. Not the office. His residence. Unlisted? Look, you don't have to give me the number. Just connect me," I pleaded, knowing it was futile. "All right, all right," I cut into her practiced spiel. "Get me the police. Sheriff's station in Oro."

When the duty officer answered, I said, "Let me speak to Sheriff Bell."

"Sorry, he's not in."

"Where is he? I have to talk to him. It's an emergency."

"What's the nature of your emergency, ma'am?"

I thought I recognized the voice, and I sure as hell didn't want to explain to him. "Get me through to Bell," I said. "Somebody else is going to die unless you do."

"Mrs. West? Is that you?"

I'd been right. Smiley.

The harsh voice crackled over the wire. "Listen, you crazy broad, you want me to lose my job? Bell's so pissed he wouldn't give you the time of day, much less—"

"Listen to me," I shouted. "There's a killer walking around over there and—"

"You're wasting my time, lady. We got real emergencies here, so go bug somebody else."

"Wait! He's got Janet Valek. You have to—" The

disconnect buzzed in my ear. The son of a bitch had hung up on me.

Rita, maybe she could—no, it would take too long to explain things, and anyway, I doubted she would have any more effect on Smiley than I had.

I flipped the receiver hook up and down until the operator came on the line. "Philip Hunter," I said. "I want to call Philip Hunter in Oro. No, I don't have any change to deposit. Make it collect."

He answered on the first ring. "Yes? Who is it?" He quickly agreed to accept the call and said, "Delilah?"

"Thank God I found you at home," I said. "I don't have time to explain this, Philip, but Janet's alive." He sputtered questions, but I said, "Just shut up and do what I tell you. She's out at Greg Adams's ranch. I'm at least an hour away. I called the police but they've decided I'm some kind of nut. Maybe they'll believe you. Janet's life depends on it, so convince them somehow. Get them out there right away."

"All right. I don't pretend to understand, but I'll do what you say. Delilah, just in case, why don't you meet me at Greg's place?"

"Tell me where it is."

"Go straight ahead past the turnoff for Mesquite Canyon. You can't miss it. The road ends at the ranch."

MIRACULOUSLY, TRAFFIC THINNED and I raced through the growing twilight toward Oro. I hoped for a police car. The C.H.P. or the sheriff's patrol. I'd let them chase me. Lead them right to Greg's doorstep. But I didn't see a single black and white during the trip.

I kept hearing Hodge's voice as he remembered his sexual attack on Janet. And Valek—he could explain away his actions any way he wanted. I knew exactly what he'd done. He'd seen a chance to make a fortune and he'd grabbed it, ruthlessly using his own daughter as a pawn. Hodge must have hated and feared him, but over the years the relationship spawned a strange kind of dependency that bound the two men together.

Janet had been caught between them. I could imagine her own fear and hatred. God knows it explained her erratic behavior—the escape into drugs and promiscuity. But why, suddenly, had she decided to tell David and Emily Hodge? To extract a final payment for all the years of pain?

Something's missing, I thought, but there was no time to figure out what it was.

I'd estimated an hour but it was forty minutes later when I sped through town and turned on the canyon road. I had to ease off the accelerator slightly when I left the asphalt. Still, the Pinto lurched and bounced, axles shivering. I clenched my teeth and fought the vibrating steering wheel. Waves of agony shot up my arm, alternating ice with fire. It didn't matter. I hurt so much inside I could barely tell where one pain left off and the other began.

Two miles past the turnoff, a grove of live oak shaded a small house, a larger barn. Rail fences enclosed a corral. Three Appaloosas drank from a trough, lifting graceful heads to watch as I parked on a graveled area midway between house and barn.

No police cars. They've come and gone, I decided, taking Janet away to safety. There was just Philip's green Seville, its windows reflecting the orangy glow of a fiery sunset. He must have waited for me. He wasn't outside, so I assumed he was in the house. I reached for the door handle, then stopped.

When I'd called Philip, my only concern had been for Janet. I'd told him nothing at all about my suspicions concerning Greg.

My God, I thought, fear coiling like a snake in my chest. If Greg was here when Philip came—no, that was crazy. Philip knew nothing. Anyway, the police were with him.

Still. . . I unlocked the glove compartment, took out the gun, and slipped it into my oversize handbag. A horse whickered as I followed a graveled walk up to the front door. The house was old but well-kept, new paint on the rough siding and a clump of bright zinnias by the front step. I knocked and the door swung open.

"Delilah," Philip said. "You made good time. Come on in and tell me what's going on."

"Did the police take Janet into town? Was Greg here when they arrived?"

"Philip? Who's at the door?" a voice called from the back of the house. A clear, feminine voice.

The front door opened directly into a living room that was gloomy with approaching darkness. Light spilled through an arched doorway in the back of the room. Beyond it, I could see an eating area and glimpse a kitchen.

"Philip?" the woman called again.

Light footsteps sounded on the tiled floor and somebody came from the kitchen and stood there, framed by the open doorway.

It was Janet Valek.

18

AFTER ALL MY EFFORTS, Janet had not been taken to a safe place. I turned on Philip, anger and frustration edging the words that I tried to keep at a whisper. "What is she doing here? Where are the police?"

"I had the same problem you did," he said. "They just wouldn't listen."

"Well, you should have taken her out of here on your own. I told you—"

"Philip?" Janet said sharply.

"It's all right, Janet. It's Mrs. West." He brushed against me as he pushed the door shut, my handbag acting like a bumper between us.

"Let's have some light in here," Janet said. "I can't see a thing."

She moved toward us, switching on lamps that stood on end tables next to a sofa, and the room sprang to life. The furniture was old, comfortably overstuffed in warm shades of brown and orange, the walls were paneled in maple. Books overflowed open shelves and joined piles of magazines and newspapers on a large coffee table. It was an intimate, cozy room. It hurt me to look at it and picture Greg here.

Janet turned on a floor lamp a few feet away, straightened and stared at me. Puzzlement turned to recognition as Philip said, "Janet, this is Delilah West."

I'd pictured her lying in a shallow grave, flesh rotting off her bones. But she was definitely alive. A little thinner, with a kind of fragility that accentuated the elegance of her slender body. Honey-colored hair was piled on top of her head, secured by combs. Violet shadows had deepened in her eyes.

"I know you," she said. "I didn't remember the name, but now I remember that we've met before. You're Rita's friend."

"Yes," I said. "So maybe you'll believe me when I tell you that we've got to get out of here. I don't know how much Philip has told you—"

"Nothing yet," Philip put in quickly. "You really didn't say what was wrong so I thought it was best to wait. I didn't want to scare her."

"What are you two talking about? Philip said you sent him here, Delilah. How did you know where I was?"

"Janet, I don't have time to explain this to you. Just take my word for it when I say you're in a great deal of danger. We have to leave now."

"This is crazy," she said. "I'm not going anywhere until you tell me what's going on."

I moved to the window, searching the gathering darkness for the flash of a headlight coming down the long stretch of dirt road. There were three of us and I was armed, but a sense of danger covered me like a second skin, a skin flayed and raw with every nerve ending exposed.

"What time does Greg get home?" I asked.

"He's usually here by now, but a client down in Warner Springs called and insisted on seeing him

tonight. Why? Has something happened to Greg?
What *is* it?''

"Janet, I want you to come with me. We'll get in
my car and go someplace where you'll be safe. I'll
tell you everything on the way.''

"No," she said emphatically. "I know why you're
here. Philip said you're working for my father. He
sent you. I should've known Dan would call him.
This place you want to take me—what'll it be this
time? Bars on the windows or doctors who smile at
you all the time they're shooting you full of tran-
quilizers?''

"You know your father pretty well," I said. "He
might have tried something like that, but not now.
Daniel Hodge is dead.''

"Dead." She said it as though I'd told her the man
had gone for an evening stroll. "Yes, well, I have
something on the stove. I'd better check on it.''

She bolted from the room and Philip started after
her.

"Wait a minute," I said.

"Did you see her face? She needs me. Jesus, that
was a cold thing to do. Why did you just drop something like that on her?''

"Shock therapy," I said wearily. It occurred to
me that if I didn't take something for the pain in
my arm and shoulder pretty soon, I might not make
it out of here standing up. "Look, Philip, I need
to talk to Janet alone. There are some very personal things I have to discuss with her. She may
want to tell you about it sometime, but that's got to
be her decision. Give me a few minutes and I'll convince her we have to leave.''

"First I want to know who's a threat to Janet. Is it
Greg?''

"Yes. Now, please, wait outside. Keep a lookout for his car just in case he didn't go to Warner Springs. I'll make this as quick as possible."

He agreed reluctantly and left me to face Janet. She was at the stove, stirring a pot with methodical concentration as though it was the only thing she had to do in the world, and she was determined to do a perfect job. She didn't look up as I filled a glass at the sink, fumbled open a pill bottle.

There was a breakfast bar at the end of the horseshoe-shaped kitchen counter, with a couple of high stools tucked under it on the dining-room side. I sat on one, swallowed two Darvon. The air was thick with the heavy odor of meat simmering with onions and cloves.

"Janet," I said. "We have to talk now. There's not much time."

She dropped the pot lid with a little crash and put down the spoon before she turned around. Her face was very pale, the blue eyes like dark smudges in a child's drawing.

"I don't feel anything," she said. "Isn't that strange? I hated him for so long, wished him dead so many times and now.... Why did my father send you here?"

"He didn't," I said. "Your father may be paying the bill, but I'm really working for your brother. He's worried sick about you."

"David? I thought I'd be back before he came home. Poor lamb, I didn't mean to upset him. But I knew it was the best thing for both of us in the long run."

As she spoke, she opened a cupboard and took out cans of vegetables, potatoes from a bin. She rummaged in a drawer for a knife, spread a paper towel on the counter between us. The knife was too big but she used it anyway, awkwardly removing the skin from the potato in large chunks.

"Janet, stop that and listen to me. I don't have time for all the niceties; so I'm going to be blunt. I know what Hodge did to you."

The knife clattered from her hands. "You mean what he tried to do three weeks ago."

"Yes, that, and about another night when you were thirteen years old."

"God," she whispered. "I think I'd better sit down."

I guided her over to the table, pulled out a chair, sat next to her. "I don't know what brought on this confrontation between you and Hodge. Whatever it was, it started a chain of violence that isn't over yet."

"You keep talking about violence and some sort of danger to me. But Dan is dead. Who else wants to hurt me?"

"The man who killed Emmy and Felix."

"Killed? No, you're wrong. Emmy—it was an accident, and Felix. . . ."

"I know what Greg's told you, Janet, but I was there both times. I dragged Emmy from the house and this—" I pulled up my sleeve and showed her the bandage around my upper arm. "Somebody shot me last night just after Felix was killed. I know they were both murdered because of what they knew about you and Daniel Hodge."

"Don't say that." Anger made hard red splotches on her cheeks. "I don't believe you. I don't believe any of this."

I wanted to shake her out of sheer frustration. I wondered if I could convince Philip to take her out of the house by force. I touched the hard outline of the gun in my purse, but dismissed the idea. The only weapon I had was words. Words she didn't want to hear.

"Hodge told me somebody helped him," I said. "I didn't just make it up."

She shook her head. "It was my phone call. He thought I was dead. I can imagine what it did to him."

"He was in pretty bad shape," I admitted.

"So he might have said anything. Maybe you misunderstood. What happened to him? Was it his heart?"

"I don't know for sure. I think so."

"I killed him, then," she said dully. "My phone call. . . . All your suspicions are wrong, Delilah, I'm the only murderer here."

"Stop that," I said. "He's to blame, not you. My God, what do I have to do to make you see—think about it for a minute. Emmy knew about you and Hodge. He paid her off to keep the secret."

"Yes, but it's not the way you make it sound. She was desperate at the time and she felt badly about it all these years. But I'm glad she took it. It was one of the few good things they ever did with their stinking money."

"She was the reason you came to Oro," I said. "It had nothing to do with Felix Bak."

"Of course. I wanted to be near Emmy to convince her to help me, so I used Felix to throw my father off the track. But I never told Felix anything about Dan. So you're wrong, Delilah. About Emmy and about Felix. There was no reason for him to be killed."

"It's true he didn't know what happened in the

past," I said. "But he drove by your house that night and he saw Hodge's car. He tried to blackmail him. I think Hodge was in over his head by then. He didn't want Felix killed, but it was out of his hands. His accomplice had to protect himself."

"You keep saying accomplice. Who?"

"The man who brought you here."

"Greg?" she asked, stunned. "That's totally insane. How can you possibly think that Greg could do something like that?"

"He must have walked in on Hodge just after he hit you," I went on relentlessly. "Maybe he overheard your conversation, enough of it to figure out what was going on, or maybe Emmy confided in him. Either way, he saw a chance to make a big score. He offered to help Hodge, to get rid of your body for him. When he discovered you were still alive, he brought you here. He didn't really want you dead, and anyway it served the same purpose if he could just keep you quiet."

"You're wrong, completely wrong. That's not how it happened at all." She jumped up and paced the narrow space between the table and counter with growing agitation. The small room was filled with the hot, sickening smell of the stew.

She stopped, braced herself against the counter. "Dan put me in the trunk of my car and left it at Felix's place. When I woke up, it was dark and I could barely move or breathe. I kept blacking out and I was so weak and scared, but I banged on the trunk lid and screamed for help. Greg heard me."

"Why was he there?"

"He was out horseback riding. He knew Felix was going away for a couple of days, so he decided to check on the dog. When he found me, he wanted to take me to Dr. Jessup and call the sheriff, but I begged him to just get me away. He took me to a hospital in Riverside, and I made him promise to keep it a secret. I couldn't have it all come out, not like that. He agreed to go back to the house and pack my things. He told Emmy part of it, but he didn't want to upset her by telling her the whole ugly thing."

"Hold it a minute," I said, with a dizzy feeling of disorientation. It was like getting up in the middle of the night and trying to walk around in the dark, only to find that somebody has rearranged all the furniture while you were asleep. "If Hodge thought you were dead, you had to be out cold, so you don't really know who put you in that trunk."

"I know it wasn't Greg. He let me stay here. He took care of me."

"Convenient," I said. "Why do you suppose he did that?"

"Because I had no place to go. It was all against his better judgment, Delilah. He kept telling me I ought to call Dan."

"And why didn't you? My God, you let the man think he'd murdered you."

"I needed time to think, to decide what to do. And I really didn't care if Dan suffered. I wanted to punish him. I wanted him to die a thousand times inside his mind, just like I have. Then, when Emmy died, I lost all hope for a while. As long as I had a witness, I could tell David the truth and they couldn't do anything to stop me."

"Tell David?" I thought about how much David loved his sister and I felt a little sick. "Is that how you planned to get back at your father, by turning David against him?"

She flinched as though I'd slapped her. "Don't look like that. You said you knew what happened to me, but you can't know." She came back and sat down, her shoulders bowed. "What happened that night eighteen years ago was only the beginning."

I understood then and reached for her hands, gripping them hard as if some of the pain could flow across the link they made. "David," I said simply.

"He's my son." The words shuddered up from some buried depths of agony. "The attack itself was horrible, but then . . . then I discovered I was pregnant."

"You were only thirteen and the victim of a rape. Even though the abortion laws hadn't been liberalized, surely—"

She shook her head. "My father wouldn't hear of it. It was morally wrong, he said. God! He never had a moral scruple in his life. The baby was going to give him a lifetime hold on Dan. That's what he wanted. Mom pleaded with him, but it didn't do any good, and then it was too late. I was too far along. So we went and stayed with Emmy and pretended that mom had a baby, that David was my brother."

"And that's why you've stayed with your father all these years."

"I had to. After mom died—he killed her, you know. She wasn't strong and living with the awful knowledge day after day, her heart gave out. I had to stay for David's sake. Before he was born I thought I'd hate him, but I never did. I've always loved him."

"Then why tell him something that will disrupt his life and cause him so much pain?"

"Because they're taking him away from me. The school back east, the summer in Europe—it's only the beginning. I'm just his sister. Sisters don't count for much, Delilah. I could see David slipping away from me and becoming like them. I couldn't stand it, that's all. Damn," she said, pulling her hands away to draw her thumbs under her eyes and wipe away an overflow of tears.

I took out some Kleenex and handed it to her. While she dried her eyes, I tried to put my thoughts back into order. I'd been so drawn into the drama of Janet's past, that the sense of danger had drifted away. It rushed back and stamped around on my backbone with icy feet.

"Listen," I said, "It's clear to me now why all this happened. But that night after Hodge hit you and you fell, there was somebody who helped him. There had to be. He wasn't strong enough to do it by himself."

"Not Greg," Janet said.

"All right. Maybe. But if it wasn't Greg, it had to be somebody else."

"Clever of you," a voice said mockingly from the doorway behind me. "It took you long enough to figure that much out. Stay very still, Delilah, and keep your hands where I can see them. Janet will tell you I have a gun, and it's pointed at the base of your skull."

19

JANET LOOKED OVER MY SHOULDER, her eyes widening in terror. All my digging, all my brilliant deductions—it had led me to Janet but to the wrong conclusions about the killer. I recognized the voice and it wasn't Greg that stood behind me. A thrill of pure joy shot through me before the sick feeling of betrayal returned.

"Good old Philip," I said bitterly. "What happened to all your loving concern?"

"Shut up," he said. "I don't like this, but there's nothing I can do about it. Now move. Both of you, over there against the counter."

I stood up slowly, my heart pumping hard. My purse was on the table, the zipper still open. Should I take a chance on going for the gun? He'd try to take me out first. If he succeeded, if I couldn't stop him, Janet would be next. But if I didn't risk it, he'd kill us both anyway. I put my hands on the edge of the table as if to steady myself, touched the leather strap.

"Keep away from the purse," Philip warned. "Leave it right where it is."

I hesitated too long for his taste. He closed the distance between us and rammed a gun barrel against my spine. I caught the smell of something sharp and acrid clinging to his clothes.

"Try me," he said savagely, "I know what you're carrying in that handbag, Delilah. You'll never get to it before I pull this trigger."

I remembered the awkward little ballet at the front door when he let me in, his stumble and the way he brushed up against me, checking me out, of course. So he knew about the revolver. Slowly, I moved my fingers away from the purse, let go of the table. Fear evaporated all the moisture from the mucous lining of my mouth and throat as I suddenly identified the odor that clung to him. It was the smell of gasoline.

He prodded me and said, "Move."

I walked the few steps to join Janet at the counter, turned around to face him. He had a rifle in his hands. He tucked it under his right arm and held it ready to fire while he upended my purse with his free hand. The gun slid out on the table. He picked it up, thumbed open the firing chamber and shook the bullets out. Then he threw the revolver into the living room.

Beside me Janet's chalky skin seemed to have shrunk over her facial bones, accenting the enormous eyes as she pleaded, "Please, Philip, don't do this."

"Sorry, love. I wish it could've been different."

"But, why?" she asked. "Tell me why."

"Ask Delilah. She has all the answers. Too bad she didn't add them up right the first time."

"He's broke," I said to Janet. "I'm sure he recognized your name when he first met you. He wanted to marry you. Isn't that right, Philip?"

Stall. Keep him talking. Greg might come home. Don't think about what Philip's been doing with gasoline.

"Sure," he said. "Only it wasn't just the money, Janet. I really was attracted to you. But you were all wrapped up in something else and you kept putting me off. Of course I didn't know what it was at the time, but it was frustrating as hell. I decided to step up my efforts. I dropped by to invite you for dinner, and I saw that big black Lincoln on your driveway. I almost left. I don't know why I didn't. Maybe I just wanted to size up any new rival. When I got to the door, it was ajar. I heard the two of you arguing. I decided to rush in and hustle him out, but just then he hit you. I opened the door and saw you fall. Your head hit the edge of the coffee table. I ran in and pushed him away, but I couldn't find a pulse and you weren't breathing. I thought you were dead, Janet. I swear I did."

"Why didn't you call the police?" Janet asked.

"The old man stopped blubbering long enough to tell me who he was and to beg for my help. I recognized his name and I knew I could get enough out of him for a fresh start. You have to understand how it was. The development is folding, Janet. I was going to lose everything."

"So you put Janet in the trunk of her car and drove it out to Bak's place with Hodge following," I said. "You planned to pin her murder on Felix, didn't you?"

"It was perfect. It should have worked. She'd dumped him and he had a reputation for violence. I knew he was going out of town for a day or two, so—"

"But Greg found Janet, and when you went into your frantic act for the police, the car was gone along with her body. It must have driven you and Hodge crazy trying to figure out what happened to it."

"Bak was already home by the time I convinced Bell to investigate," he said. "When the police didn't find anything, I decided Felix must have discovered the body, that maybe he figured he really had killed her while he was high. He was scared, so he got rid of the body and the car, packed her belongings so it looked like she left town."

"Meantime Hodge was on your back," I prompted.

"I'd convinced him we were in the clear, but then he called and said the Valeks had hired you to check up on Janet."

"So you had to look properly grief stricken and miserable for my sake," I said. "I always thought you weren't quite as drunk as you pretended, Philip. You played me like a pro, leading me to Janet's house so I'd find Emmy. You went straight there from the restaurant, didn't you? Was it hard murdering that helpless old lady?"

"It had to be done. She knew about Janet and Hodge. Now that's enough conversation." His long fingers moved nervously over the rifle stock. "I know what you're trying to do, Delilah, and it won't work. Greg won't be home for hours. He's off on a wild-goose chase to Warner Springs. I made sure of that. So stalling won't help."

"Philip, please." Janet held out a supplicating hand and took a step forward. "How can you do this? If it's money you want, my father will pay. Let me call him. I'm sure that he . . . . ."

"Stay right there," he barked. "I've got enough money from Hodge to start over. But it won't do me any good if I go to jail for murder."

"But you can't just . . . . My God, Delilah, he's going to kill us."

She pressed against me and I could feel her whole body trembling. "Take it easy," I said, turning to her. I slipped my right arm around her in what I hoped looked like a gesture of comfort. My heart thumped painfully, playing my ribs like a xylophone.

"But he wouldn't tell us all this unless he—"

"No need to panic," I said soothingly, using her body as a shield as I fumbled blindly on the counter behind her for something to use as a weapon.

If I could just reach the knife—Janet had been using it to peel potatoes. Only what good would it do at this distance against a rifle? To hell with logic. It was something, a chance. Where had she put it? I couldn't find the damn thing without an obvious movement.

"Move over," Philip said sharply. "Get your hands back where I can see them."

"I'm trying to help Janet," I said. "Look at her. She's shaking like a leaf. She'll collapse."

"No, she won't. Get away from her or I'll—"

"You'll what? Shoot us? Somehow I don't think so. The sheriff would have a hard time swallowing a couple of bullet-riddled corpses as an accident. That's what you're planning, isn't it? An accident. How about a brush fire? That ought to do the job nicely."

Janet gasped. "Fire? Oh, no, Philip. You wouldn't do that—please...."

"Of course not. Don't listen to her," he said, but I looked into his eyes and knew I was right.

"He's lying," I said. "You can smell the gasoline on his clothes."

I scrabbled frantically and my fingers closed around a can. Peas. I remembered seeing the label clearly as Janet took it from the cupboard.

"Sometimes you're too smart for your own good, Delilah," Philip said. "Do as I say. Push me and I can always change my mind and shoot you. Now move!"

I did, but the movement was not what he expected. I shoved Janet hard and she cried out, staggering away. I threw the can at Philip and dived for the floor. His yelp of surprise was drowned out by the boom of the rifle going off.

A great roar stabbed my eardrums and then a flash of white-hot pain exploded above my right eye. The room filled with blinding light and fragmented images, chiaroscuro, fiercely bright for an instant then doing a slow fade into darkness. I heard sounds but they were meaningless, mixed with echoes from the gunfire, growing farther and farther away.

Time stopped. A month went by, or was it hours? Maybe a minute. I couldn't tell. My first sensation was the rough texture of floor tile against my cheek. I was in a kitchen with strong odors of cooking bearing down oppressively. I remembered that. Not much more. My head felt as though somebody had filled it with Jell-O. Screams sliced it into quivering globs.

Janet. Janet was screaming.

I bent my elbows, brought my hands up level with my breasts. Put my palms flat against the floor. Pushed. Lashes of pain struck in stinging blows. I couldn't tell which hurt the most, my head or my shoulder. I was upright finally, but almost immediately I started to topple over again. Caught myself against something solid. Wood. The cabinet base at the bottom of the cupboards.

Hoarse cries rang out. A crash near by. More screams.

"Janet," I mumbled, but I couldn't see her.

I couldn't see anything. The explosion and the pain—blind—I was blind. I clawed at my eyes. Found bone and skin all intact, but covered in sticky wetness. I rubbed hard and with an effort pulled my eyelids apart. Blood had gummed them together. More ran down. I blinked, tried to brush it away.

The bullet had hit me in the forehead. No. That was crazy. I'd be dead. Maybe I fell, banged my head. It didn't matter. I could see now, a fuzzy image growing steadily clearer.

I saw Janet and Philip, locked together, reeling, her arms clamped around his neck, her feet off the floor as he swung her around, staggering, trying to shake her loose.

There was no gun in his hand. Where was the gun? I had to find it. More blood in my eyes—can't see—where is it?

On my hands and knees, I scanned the floor, but another scream from Janet snapped my head up just as Philip slammed her against the wall. Her arms fell away from his neck and she slid to the floor. He reached for her, put his hand around her throat.

I half ran, half crawled toward him, tackled him waist high. The force of my body sent him sprawling.

"Janet," I croaked. "Get up. Hurry. The gun...."

She didn't move. I could hear her breathe in harsh, straining gulps. Philip got to his feet slowly. I backed toward the counter. Behind strands of lank black hair, his eyes fastened on my face. They were so black the pupils blended with the irises. Light glittered on the surface, creating facets like the eyes of some monstrous insect advancing on its prey.

I inched down the counter, gagging on the scent of my own blood combined with the nauseous odor of stew. If only I could reach the pot, throw the boiling contents in his face, but it was on the other wall of the horseshoe-shaped counter. I'd never get to it in time. No, it had to be the knife. Where the hell was it? *Think.* Janet had dropped it. So it must be there. Somewhere in the potato peelings.

I tensed, whirled, saw it. Clenched the handle in my fist, but he was on me just as I turned, pinning me down, his fingers closing around my wrist.

His other hand dug into the wound in my left shoulder. Great bouts of pain sprouted up, spreading like flame deep into my bones, turning muscles and sinew into strings of fire, exploding red-hot pinpoints of light across my vision. A scream echoed inside my head, and dimly I realized that the sound was coming from my own lips.

I bit down hard, chopping the howl into a guttural moan. Focused my eyes to look into the manic blackness only inches away.

His body was hard against mine, forcing me backward, the edge of tiled counter crushing my spine. Any more pressure and the vertebra might crack. Miraculously, the knife was still in my hand. Through all the pain I'd hung on to it, locking my fingers like a death grip around the handle.

"Drop it," Philip said.

I tried to twist away and screamed, "Janet! Janet, get the rifle. Help me!"

She lay against the far wall and she didn't respond. Philip squeezed my shoulder again.

"She can't help you," he said. "Do what I say. Drop the knife or . . . ."

The pressure increased, each finger like a gigantic hammer driving spikes into my flesh. I felt reality shudder and begin to slide away.

I reached for anger and held on tight. "You bastard," I gasped.

I wanted to tear out his eyes. Smash my knee into his balls. Cripple him. Maim him. Kill the son of a bitch. But I was pinned between his legs. Helpless. Except . . . .

With one final effort I lifted my head and sank my teeth into his cheek. The skin ripped and I tasted blood. I bit deeper in a savage tearing motion. The black eyes bulged, strained wide open, full of stunned horror. It was his turn to scream, a hoarse cry of agony rumbling up from his chest.

His body went slack for an instant. I was ready for it, twisting away. I didn't get far. Roaring with pain, he grabbed for me. But this time the knife was between us. It struck his rib cage, found an opening, went in, came out again. I couldn't tell how far it penetrated because the shock of steel hitting bone sent the knife clattering from my numb fingers.

We stood there, facing each other, swaying. A red stain blossomed on his shirt. He touched it, stared at the blood on his hand in disbelief.

Then with a terrible howl of agony and rage, he swung his fist toward my face.

I fell down a long dark shaft, angling into blackness.

20

I WAS AT THE BOTTOM OF A WELL and somebody was nailing down the cover. Faint streaks of light only intensified the blackness. I scrabbled for handholds on slick, hard walls, knew I was going nowhere. I was trapped. I fought anyway, clawing my way upward.

Outside, a long way off, somebody called my name. I strained toward the sound and it grew clearer.

"Delilah? Oh, my God, Delilah, wake up. Please wake up."

Janet's voice, thick with hysteria.

Opening my eyes was the hardest thing I'd ever done. The lids weighed a hundred pounds each and drying blood glued the lashes shut. I couldn't see her even after I pried them open. All I saw was the doorway, the edge of the living-room carpet.

"Jesus, help me," Janet cried. "She has to wake up. Delilah!"

"Okay," I said, or thought I said, but no words came out. I tried again. "It's okay. I hear you."

"Thank God you're alive." She sobbed in relief, fought for control so she could continue. "Philip—he's outside. He's going to do it. A fire . . . fire . . . ." Her voice squeezed off in terror.

"Help me," I said. "I can't seem to move."

"I can't. He tied me up. Hurry, Delilah."

With an enormous effort I turned my head toward the sound of her voice. She was in a chair, arms bound behind her with kitchen towels. Feet tied together. I moved my own arms tentatively. They were free. Probably thought I was dead so he didn't bother to tie me up. He had a lot to learn about how much it takes to kill somebody.

"How long," I croaked. "How long since he went outside?"

I couldn't get up. My body felt like it had come out of a spray can. I dragged it inch by inch toward the chair.

"I don't know," Janet said. "It seems like forever, but I guess it was only minutes. Oh, God, I thought he'd killed you. Please . . . we've got to get out of here. He's crazy. He must be to do something like this."

I picked at the knot in the towel with fingers that felt like they belonged in a frying pan instead of on my hands. "I had a knife. I'm sure I stabbed him. I think there was a lot of blood."

"There was but it didn't stop him." The knot loosened. She pulled her arms free and worked frantically on the towel that bound her feet. It fell away and she stood up. "Come on, Delilah."

"I don't think I can get up."

"Yes, you can. I'll help you."

She grabbed my wrists, pulled. Somehow I was on my feet, staggering, her arm around my waist for support.

"Lean on me," she said. "We can make it."

"Wait. If he's out there. . . ." I couldn't finish the thought. My mind felt as though somebody had worked it over with a paper punch, cutting out big

chunks of logic and memory. Nothing made any
sense.

"We have to go now," she said, terror edging her
voice. The combs were gone and hair tangled
around her face. Her eyes were swollen, her skin
bruised and blotchy from weeping. "For God's
sake, we're going to die in here. Can't you smell it?
It's smoke."

"But there's something—" I mumbled, my feet
following her lead as she dragged me through the
living room toward the front door. "Not this way,"
I said. "The back door."

She ignored me and we stumbled outside. Dry hot
air with just a trace of evening coolness rushed over
me. "No smoke," I said. "Where's the smoke?"

"I don't know." Confusion was plain in her voice.
"I thought—I could've sworn . . . ."

Fear cleared the numbness that paralyzed my
thoughts. "He heard us," I said. "He's waiting. For
Christ's sake, get us back inside."

"No," she said, panicked. "I won't be trapped in
there."

"We can use the telephone. Get help."

"We can't. I got to it before he grabbed me that
last time. The line is dead."

"The gun, then." My mind was working now. It
was only my body that was useless. "Did he have
the rifle when he went outside?"

"I don't know. I don't think so. No."

"You have to get it," I said. "Janet, I can't do it,
so leave me here and go back for it."

"No, I can't." The words were a terrified sob.
"We'll get to the car. We'll get away."

I thought of the enormous distance between us
and the parking area. I strained to see something in

the growing darkness. The last rays of sunlight gave the world an eerie look, a reddish monotone quickly changing to shades of gray. There was a scent of dust and hay and horse dung, but over it all was the acrid odor of gasoline.

Philip. He was out there somewhere. He had to be. Unless he'd changed his mind. Run away. Maybe he was halfway to the Mexican border. But no, there were two cars parked in the graveled area next to the barn. I could see their boxy rooflines, the long snouts of hood.

"Delilah, please," Janet whispered, tugging, pulling me with her.

She was beyond reason, so I said, "All right. We'll have to take a chance. I left the keys in my car. Help me."

We began our slow, agonizingly slow, retreat. Was Janet right about the rifle? What if Philip did have it? My body quivered with the expectation of a sudden hail of bullets. The fear stimulated my adrenal glands. By the time we got to the car, the horrible weakness had ebbed and my legs felt firm again. A little wobbly, but they worked. I leaned against the roof while Janet reached for the door to let me in on the passenger's side.

"Get in," she said. "Hurry."

I saw a blur of movement a split second before she opened the door. Light spilled out, cutting through the darkness, pinning him like a blood-smeared moth. He was sitting about ten feet away in a strip of dry grass that lay between the horse corral and the parking area.

"Janet," I said. "He's there. Janet—"

He tried to get up but sank back down again. Next to me, Janet whimpered deep in her throat.

"Easy," I said. "I don't see a gun. He's hurt. I don't think he can move very fast. Slide in from this side and get the engine started."

She slipped quickly into the driver's seat. I heard her engage the ignition, but I kept my eyes on Philip as I lowered myself into the car. The only sound from the starter was a dull clicking.

"Oh, God," she said. "Oh, no. Please...."

There was nothing, but she kept turning the key. I put my hand over hers to stop her. "It's no good. He must have disabled it. Probably the rotor. We'll have to try for the Seville. But first, turn on the headlights."

"What?"

"The headlights. Turn them on. So we can see what he's doing."

The flood of light caught him on all fours looking for something. On the other side of the rail fence, two of the Appaloosas stamped nervously, their spotted haunches ghostly white.

"We've got to get back to the house," I said.

We got out of the car but it was too late. He found what he was looking for. Janet had been wrong. He did have the rifle. The barrel swung up.

"Stay there." His voice was thick, almost unrecognizable. "Get back in the car."

"Philip," I said. "You're hurt. You need a doctor. Put down that gun and let us help you."

"No—not the way I planned it...have to...." He fumbled in his pocket. Light glittered on a small metallic object.

"Philip, listen to me," I said. But he was beyond listening.

"Delilah, what is he doing?" Janet asked.

I saw the yellow flicker and I screamed, "No! Philip, the gasoline—"

Fire ran up his arms like a torch. It danced briefly like a halo around his face before it leaped to his hair. He was all rounded mouth and popping eyes, a soundless terror that gave way to a scream that shattered the night with horror.

Janet was screaming, too, and the horses added high-pitched whinnies as they reared away from the flames and pawed the air. He stood up, gyrating, beating futilely at his body. I ran toward him, but the grass ignited with a whoosh, shooting flames skyward. Through an orange inferno, I saw him jerk, puppetlike, and fall.

The fire streaked toward the barn. There was no way I could get to Philip. Nothing I could do if I reached him. I ran back to Janet who stood rooted in horror. Shook her roughly.

"The whole place is going," I said. "We have to get out of here. Maybe Philip's car—"

"No!" She pulled away and ran for the house.

"Janet! For God's sake, come back here. Wait."

I thought she'd gone crazy. At the corner of the house she dropped down on her knees. Then I heard a hissing sigh and realized what she was doing. Sprinklers came on around the edge of the yard.

"Get the hose," she gasped. "It's right here. Wet down the roof. I have to go to the horses."

Before I could stop her, she was running toward the corral. I scrabbled in the darkness for the faucet and the coil of hose that was already connected. I turned it on full blast, drenching myself in the process. The odor of gasoline was so strong here that I gagged on it. If one spark struck, it would be all over. I tried to wash it away before I turned the water toward the roof.

Waves of smoke stung my eyes and filled my lungs. The fire made a singing, crackling sound. Streaming tears and coughing, I called, "Janet? Janet?"

The barn went up in a roar, shooting orange jets high into the air. I pictured her turned to a human torch like Philip, burning to a blackened lump out there in that holocaust, but suddenly she was beside me, gasping for air and choking out, "Can't save the barn. Opened the gate. The horses... free...."

We didn't say anything else. We couldn't. It took all our strength to draw enough oxygen to keep us alive as we fought the rain of flying embers.

The barn went quickly, the walls tilting crazily and the roof falling in. But the wind was with us, carrying the fire away. It raced southward through the dry brush toward the horizon.

"Keep the water going," Janet said hoarsely. "Got to get a blanket. Beat out the sparks."

We worked steadily, flinching from every noisy growl in the mass of glowing timbers, stamping out each new spit of fire.

Finally it was over. The barn was a smoldering pile of rubble. Far away, sirens wailed.

"'Bout time," I mumbled, dropping down beside Janet. We sat with our backs against the side of the house near the front door and waited.

"Philip," she numbly.

"No use. He's dead, Janet. There's nothing we can do for him."

She lifted a soot-stained face. "We saved the house."

"You saved it. I'd have given up. But you worked like a madwoman."

"I couldn't let it be destroyed. Greg loves this place. At least I salvaged something. All the rest—oh, God, Delilah, will it all come out now? The murders. . . David. . . ." The words choked off.

"I think it depends on you," I said. "This could look like just what Philip planned—a brush fire. And I imagine your father is working overtime to cover up the rest of it. He's an expert at that."

"But you know what happened," she said. "Will you tell the police?"

"Strictly speaking, I should. But I won't. Not if you decide against it."

"It was my decision that started it all in the first place. How can I tell David now? I don't even know if I should tell him. If he blames me . . . ."

"I wonder if you know David at all," I said. "He's a lot stronger than you think, a lot more levelheaded. And he loves you. I'm sure of that. Maybe you ought to think about yourself. Will you be able to live with another lie? Especially this one?"

"I don't know," she whispered helplessly. "I can't decide right now. I've got to think. Maybe Greg can help me."

Greg.

A spasm twisted my insides. She had a lot of thinking to do, but so did I. Like why I'd denied all my instincts and jumped so readily to the conclusion that Greg was the murderer.

Could it be because I was so near to feeling something for him? Call it love or maybe just a very strong sexual attraction. Whatever it was, it carried the very real possibility of loss, of pain too deep to be tolerated. Had I looked for a barrier, any kind of barrier, to keep myself safe from such a risk?

God, I thought, and knew it was true.

A fire engine roared into the yard with Greg's car close behind. There was noise and confusion as the crew spilled out, but I waited for only one figure to emerge from the crowd. When he did, my heart closed up like a clenched fist, listening for the name on his lips, knowing what it would be.

"Janet," he called.

She scrambled up and ran to meet him. He folded her in his arms.

It hurt, but it wasn't nearly as bad as I expected. More like a bittersweet ache mingled with a feeling of infinite sadness.

At least Janet would be all right. She had some terrible decisions to make, but Greg would help her.

And me? I had a job. I did it. I forgot to be afraid. Rita's right. It's time to let go of the past.

Let

Raven House Mysteries

keep you in suspense!

An exciting new series
of mystery novels filled
with action and intrigue,
suspense and danger.

Raven House Mysteries let you...

- Match wits with a wily detective.
- Shudder with the hapless victim.
- Thrill to the chase.

Experience all this and
much, much more with

Raven House Mysteries...
Synonymous with the best in
crime fiction!

A Special Offer from...

Raven House Mysteries

4 Free Mystery Novels!

**That's right. You will receive
absolutely free 4 exciting new
mystery novels from RAVEN HOUSE
as your introduction to the
RAVEN HOUSE MYSTERIES subscription plan.
Your FREE books are**

Crimes Past
by Mary Challis

The embezzled half million
had disappeared into thin
air. When a corpse turned up
with a switchblade lodged
in its back, it was clear
that one of the thieves had
turned into a murderer!

Drilling for Death
John Wolfe

Someone wanted Johnny
McCoy dead. He knew too
much—about a tawdry bar,
and a regular customer who
had planted a bomb that
plunged a millionaire to his
fiery death....

Red Is for Shrouds
by Mary Ann Taylor

Someone was killing
redheaded girls. Three
of them had been savagely
bludgeoned to death, and
small-town Police Chief
Emil Martin's job was
squarely on the line.

Rain with Violence
Dell Shannon

The rain brought ugly
problems for Lt. Mendoza.
Senseless killings, suicides...
and a ruthless gang of B-girls
whose knockout drops
knocked their victims out
for good!

**Thrill to these exciting new novels
filled with action, intrigue, suspense and danger.**

RAVEN HOUSE MYSTERIES
are more than ordinary reading entertainment.

Don't miss this exciting opportunity to read, FREE, some of the very best in crime fiction.

It's a chance you can't afford to let pass by.

As a RAVEN HOUSE subscriber you will receive every month 4 thrilling new mystery novels, all written by authors who know how to keep you in suspense till the very last page.

You may cancel your subscription whenever you wish. Should you decide to stop your order, just let us know and we'll cancel all further shipments.

CLIP AND MAIL THIS COUPON TODAY!